Mrs. Hungerford

The Hoyden

Vol. II

Mrs. Hungerford

The Hoyden
Vol. II

ISBN/EAN: 9783337052928

Printed in Europe, USA, Canada, Australia, Japan

Cover: Foto ©Andreas Hilbeck / pixelio.de

More available books at **www.hansebooks.com**

THE HOYDEN

THE HOYDEN

A NOVEL

BY

MRS. HUNGERFORD

AUTHOR OF
'MOLLY BAWN,' 'THE O'CONNORS OF BALLINAHINCH,'
'NOR WIFE NOR MAID,' ETC.

IN THREE VOLUMES
VOL. II.

LONDON
WILLIAM HEINEMANN
1894

THE HOYDEN

CHAPTER XVIII.

HOW TITA GETS A SCOLDING, AND HOW SHE
REBELS AND ACCUSES SIR MAURICE OF
BREACH OF CONTRACT.

'CAN I come in ?'

Rylton's voice is a little curt as he
knocks at his wife's door. It is not the
door opening into the corridor outside, but
the inner door that leads from her room to
his, and to the dressing-room beyond.

'Yes, of course,' cries Tita pleasantly.

She is just on the point of dismissing
her maid for the night—the maid who has
so little to do ; no long hair to brush, only

the soft little curly locks that cover her mistress's head. She has taken off Tita's evening gown, and, now that the little locks have been carefully seen to, has taken off her dressing-gown also. It occurs to Tita that she might as well take *herself* off as well, and as soon as possible.

This thought makes her laugh.

'You can go now, Sarah,' says she to the maid, who loves her; 'and don't bring me my tea before eight to-morrow, because I'm as sleepy as sleepy can be.'

She nods kindly to the dismissed maid, and, going to the door where Rylton is presumably standing, lets him in.

'How early you are!' says she, thinking of the glories of the smoking-room below.

'How late you are!' returns he. 'I half fancied you would have been asleep by this time!'

'Oh, well, I soon shall be!' says she. 'I was just going to say my prayers as

you came in; after that it won't take me
a minute to get out of my clothes, and,'
with a little laugh, 'into my bed.'

Her clothes, as she stands at present,
are so becoming that it seems quite a pity
that she should ever get out of them.
Her neck and arms—soft and fair and
round as a little child's—are shining in the
lamplight, and beneath them the exquisite
lace petticoat she wears gives her the air
of one who is just going to a fancy ball.
It is short enough to show the perfect
little feet and the slender ankles beneath it.

'How inhospitable of you to desert your
friends so soon!' says she. 'Why, you
never come up till two, do you?—at least,
so you tell me.'

'You will catch cold if you stay like
that,' says he.

It is a somewhat irrelevant remark; but,
for the first time in all his knowledge of
her, the tender charm that is her own
becomes clear to him. It seems to him
that she is a new being—one he has

never seen before ; and, with this fresh
knowledge, his anger towards her grows
stronger.

'I !—in this weather ! Why, it is hardly
chilly even yet, in spite of the rain ; and,
besides, I have this fire !' She catches
his hand, and draws him towards the
hearthrug. 'I am sure you have something to say to me,' says she. 'Come and
sit by the fire, and tell me all about it.'

'It is nothing, really,' says Rylton, re-
sisting her pretty efforts to push him into
a luxurious lounging chair. 'It is only a
question about your cousin.'

He leans his elbow on the chimney-
piece, and looks down at her—a dainty
fairy lying now in the bosom of some soft
pink cushions, with her legs crossed and
her toes towards the fire. She has clasped
her arms behind her head.

'About Minnie ?'

'No.'

His heart hardens again. Is this duplicity
on her part ? How small, how innocent,

how girlish, how—reluctantly this—beautiful she looks! and yet——

'About Tom, then?'

'About Mr. Hescott'—coldly—'yes.'

'What! you don't like him?' questions
Tita, abandoning her lounging attitude,
and leaning towards him.

'So far as he is concerned,' with increasing coldness, 'I am quite indifferent
to him; it is of you I think.'

'Of me! And why of me? Why should
you think of me?'

'I hardly know,' somewhat bitterly;
'except that it is perhaps better that *I*
should criticise your conduct than—other
people.'

'I don't know what you mean!' says
Tita slowly.

Her charming face loses suddenly all its
vivacity; she looks a little sad, a little
forlorn.

'There is very little to know,' says
Rylton hurriedly, touched by her expression.

'But you said—you spoke of my *conduct !*'

'Well, and is there nothing to be said of that ? This cousin——' He stops, and then goes on abruptly : 'Why does he call you Titania ?'

'Oh, it is an old name for me !' She looks at him, and, leaning back again in her chair, bursts out laughing. She has flung her arms over her head again, and now looks at him from under one of them with a mischievous smile. 'Is *that* the whole ?' says she. 'He used to call me that years ago. He used to say I was like a fairy queen.'

'Used he ?'

Rylton's face is untranslatable.

'Yes. I was the smallest child alive, I do believe.' She springs to her feet, and goes up to Rylton in a swaying, graceful little fashion. 'I'm not so very big even *now*, am I ?' says she.

Rylton turns his eyes from hers with open determination ; he steels his heart against her.

' About this cousin,' he says icily. ' He is the one who used to say you had hands like iron, and a heart like velvet ?'

' Yes. *Fancy* you remembering that !' says Tita, a sudden, quick gleam of pleasure dyeing her pretty cheeks quite red.

' I always remember,' returns Rylton distantly.

His tone is a repulse. The lovely colour fades from her face.

' I'm tired,' says she suddenly, petulantly. She moves to the other end of the room, and, opening a wardrobe, pretends to make some re-arrangements with its contents. ' If you have nothing more to say '—with perhaps more honesty than politeness—' I wish you would go away.'

' I *have* something more to say.' The very nervousness he is feeling makes his tone unnecessarily harsh. ' I object to your extreme intimacy with your cousin.'

Tita drops the dress she has just taken from the wardrobe, and comes back once more into the full light of the lamp. Her bare and slender arms are now hanging straight before her, her fingers interlaced ; she looks up at him.

'With *Tom ?*'

' With Mr. Hescott.'

' I have known Tom all my life,' defiantly.

' I don't care about that. One may know people all one's life, and yet have very unpleasant things said about one.'

' *Can* one——' She stops suddenly, facing him, her eyes fixed on his ; her lips part, her slight little frame quivers as if with eagerness. It grows quite plain that there is something she desires passionately to say to him—something terrible—but all at once she controls herself ; she makes a little gesture with her right hand, as if throwing something from her, and goes on quickly, excitedly : ' What do you mean ? Who has been talking about me ?'

' I didn't say anyone had been talking about you.'

' Yes, you did ! You hinted it, at all events. Go on. Tell me who it was.'

'Even if I knew I should not tell you,' says Rylton, who is now white with anger.

He had understood her hesitation of a moment since. He had known exactly what she wanted to say to him, and unfortunately the pricking of his conscience had only served to add fuel to the fire of his discontent towards her.

'Well, *I'll* tell *you*,' says Tita, coming a step closer to him, her eyes blazing. 'It was Mrs. Bethune I know that she is no friend of mine. And I may as well say at once that I detest her. *You* may like her, but I don't, and I never shall. She's a *beast !*'

'Tita !'

Her husband stares at her aghast. The small form seems transfigured. Has she grown ?

'Yes—a *beast !* I don't care what you think. I'm not afraid of you—remember that ! I was not even afraid of Uncle George. I shall never be afraid of anyone in all this wide, wide world !'

Suddenly her passion breaks down. Her arms fall to her sides, and she leans back against the end of her bed like a little broken lily.

' Tita—if you would let me explain,' says Rylton, who is overcome by her forlorn attitude, ' I——'

'No.' He would have laid his hands gently upon her pretty bare shoulders, but she repulses him. ' I want no explanation ; there *isn't* one.'

Then, to his surprise and misery, she covers her face with both her hands and bursts into tears.

' You are unkind,' sobs she wildly. ' And you are not *true*. You don't tell the truth. You said—you *said*,' passionately, ' that you would be good to me. That you would let me do as I liked—that I should be happy ! That was why I married you ! That I might be happy ! And now— now——'

' But to do as you liked ! Tita, be reasonable.'

'Oh, *reasonable !* Uncle George used
to talk to me like that. *He* was a reasonable person, I suppose ; and so are you.
And he—hated me.' She grows silent as
one might when some dreadful thought
assails one. 'Perhaps,' says the poor child,
in a quick, frightened sort of way, 'you
hate me too. Perhaps everyone hates me.
There are people whom everyone hates,
aren't there ?'

'Are there ?' asks Rylton drearily.

At this moment, at all events, he feels
himself to be hateful. What a pitiful little
face he is looking at !

'Yes, my uncle detested me,' says Tita
slowly, as if remembering things. 'He
said I ought not to have had all that
money. That if I had not been born, he
would have had it. But one can't help
being born. One isn't asked about it !
If'—she pauses, and the tears well up
into her eyes again—'if *I* had been asked,
I should have said no, *no*, NO !'

'Don't talk like that,' says Rylton.

There is a sensation of chokiness about his throat. How young she is—how small —and to be *already* sorry that ever she was born! What a slender little hand! Just now it is lying crushed against her breast. And those clear eyes. Oh, if only he could have felt differently towards her—if he could have loved her! All this passes through his mind in an instant. He is even thinking of making her some kindly speech that shall heal the present breach between them, when she makes a sudden answer to his last remark.

'If you weren't here, I shouldn't have to talk at all,' says she.

'True,' he returns, feeling a little discomfited. 'Well, good-night, Tita.'

'Good-night.'

She refuses to see his proffered hand.

'Of course,' says Rylton, who now feels *he* is in the wrong, 'I am very sorry that I—that I——'

'Yes, so am I,' with a saucy little tilting of her chin.

'Sorry,' continues Rylton, with dignity, 'that I felt it my duty to—to——'

'Make a fool of yourself? *So am I!*' says Lady Rylton.

After this astounding speech there is silence for a moment or two. Then Rylton, in spite of himself, laughs. And after a faint struggle with *her*self, Tita joins in his mirth. Emboldened by this departure, and really anxious to make it up with her, Rylton bids her good-night again, and this time would have added a kiss to his adieu. But Tita pushes him away.

'Kiss you? Not likely!' says she scornfully; 'I shall never want to kiss you again in all my life!'

CHAPTER XIX.

HOW RYLTON'S HEART CONDEMNS HIM.
AND HOW, AS HE WALKS, A SERPENT
STINGS HIM. AND HOW HE IS RECOVERED
OF HIS WOUND. AND HOW THE LITTLE
RIFT IS MENDED—BUT WITH TOO FINE
THREAD.

RYLTON had gone to his own room in a strange frame of mind. He called it aggrieved, but, *au fond*, there were some grains of remorse at the bottom of it. He had married her, and in spite of all things was bound to protect her. That sad little touch of hers, 'Perhaps everyone hates me,' had gone to his heart.

There were other things that had gone

home too. Little things, but bitter to the senses of one highly cultured ; and of course the Ryltons had been accustomed to the best of things always. Tita's phrases grated a good deal. That 'make a fool of yourself' had sunk deep, and there were so many other extraordinary expressions. The women of his own world very often used them in fun, but Tita used them in earnest : that made all the difference.

And yet—he was sorry that he had vexed her. It kept him sleepless an hour almost, dwelling upon this, and even in the morning, when he awoke, it was the first thought that assailed him.

*   *   *   *   *

It is in truth a lovely morning. Sweet as June, and fresh as ' Freshë May.'

Rylton, whilst dressing, tells himself he wishes to goodness he had been clever enough to make it up with his wife before going to bed last night. Nothing so horrid as little coldnesses, little bickerings before one's guests—and Tita is so untutored that probably she will make it rather unbearable for him during breakfast.

He has underrated Tita, however. She is almost the first down, and gets through the morning salutations to her guests in the gayest style, and takes possession of the teapot and the huge old urn quite calmly. She has delivered up the coffee to Margaret, to whom she always looks as a sure ally. So calm, so pretty is her demeanour, that Rylton, taking heart of grace, throws to her a word or two—to his utter chagrin !

Not that the words are not responded to ; not one of them, indeed, but is answered, yet Tita's eyes had not gone with her words. They had been downcast; busied, presumably, with the teacup now, or a smile to her neighbour on her left, or a chiding to the fox-terrier at her knee. She gives Rylton the impression, at all events, that she will be civil to him in the future, but that she regrets the fact that she has to be.

When the hateful meal is over he rises, telling himself that he must make it up with her, and as soon as possible. That child! to have a living feud with *her*. It is out of the question! And, besides, before one's guests! How bad it will look. A disagreement is not allowed between a host and hostess—when one is staying in their house, at all events. It is quite simple to get all the quarrelling over beforehand, to so arrange as to look like winged angels when one's house-party is here to see.

He refuses to have anything to do with a swift glance from Mrs. Bethune as he leaves the breakfast-room. He gets quickly past her, disturbed at heart, and going through the hall, turns abruptly towards the stables.

The day is lovely. A sort of Indian summer reigns. And presently most of those staying in the house turn their steps towards the pleasure grounds. The tennis courts have been kept marked, in spite of the fact that the regular tennis season is at an end, and Mr. Gower, who is an indefatigable player, has called on Miss Hescott to get up a double with him.

The idea has evidently caught on, for now everyone seems to be swarming tennis-wards, rackets in hand, and tennis shoes on feet.

Rylton, turning back from the stables an hour later, and with a mind still much upset, finds all the courts occupied, and everyone very much alive. Standing on the top of the stone steps that lead down to one of the courts, he glances sharply round him. No! Tita is not here. Tita, who is a perfect devotee where tennis is concerned. Where is she, then? A second time his glance sweeps the tennis courts, and now his brow grows dark; Hescott is not here, either.

He draws in his breath a little sharply, and without descending the steps, goes round the courts nearest him to where an

opening in the wood will lead him beyond
fear of conversation.

As he reaches this opening, a voice
behind him cries gaily, 'Whither away,
Sir Maurice?'

He turns and manages to smile pleasantly at Minnie Hescott, who, with Mrs.
Bethune, is close behind him. A fancy
that Marian has brought Miss Hescott
here to say something occurs to him, and
he curses himself for the thought. Is he
growing suspicious of *everyone*?

'I was going down to one of the lower
farms,' says he in a light tone. He had
not been going there, but the evasion
seems impossible to avoid.

'You won't find anything *there*,' says
Mrs. Bethune, smiling at him. She is
dressed entirely in black, and from under
the huge black hat that shades her face
her eyes gleam up at him in a sort of
mockery—sad, yet beseeching. She is
looking beautiful! Her pale face, so
refined; the masses of her rich, red

hair shining gorgeously in the clear sunlight.

'No? I shall find old Wicks and his wife, at all events.'

'Oh, that? Yes.'

'Why, what did you think 1 was looking for?'

'I really hardly know;' she smiles, and then says quietly, 'Why, amusement, of course.'

At this moment Minnie Hescott, who detests being left out of anything, determines on boring a way into the *tête-à-tête* before her.

'Where is Tita?' asks she. 'We wanted her for tennis, she is such a good player; but no one could find her.'

'Not even your brother?' asks Mrs. Bethune.

'Not even Tom; she disappeared somewhere after breakfast.'

'Why, so did he!' and Mrs. Bethune lifts her brows in a very amused fashion.

'Oh no, he didn't,' says Minnie Hescott,

casting a sudden shrewd glance at her.
'He was in the library writing letters till
an hour ago. I know that, because I was
with him.'

'What an excellent sister you are!' says
Mrs. Bethune, with a slight laugh.

'Why?' asks Miss Hescott slowly.
'Because I was with him?' Her tone is
a little dangerous.

'Naturally,' says Mrs. Bethune, saving
herself promptly. 'To be always with
one's brother shows devotion indeed ; but
you forget your *rôle*, don't you ? Where
has he been for the past hour ? You
haven't told us that ! Surely you have
not forsaken him now, when it may be
the hour of his extremity.' Her tone is
jesting, but all through it Rylton can read
between the lines.

'He is with Colonel Neilson, at the
kennels,' replies Miss Hescott promptly.

'Ah, I told you you were a good sister,'
says Mrs. Bethune.

'Because I said Tom was with Colonel

Neilson? Do you think he *isn't* with
him?' asks Minnie, looking at her fixedly.

'My *dear* girl! What a *bêtise!* No!
Because you take such care to know what
he is doing. And so he is now with
Colonel Neilson?'

'Yes,' shortly.

'I'm afraid I must go,' says Sir Maurice;
'if I don't catch those Wickses at this hour
I shall never catch them at all.' He nods
to Minnie. For a second his eyes meet
Marian's. There is something in them
that so satisfies her, that on her way back
with Minnie she makes herself thoroughly
agreeable to that astute damsel. What *was*
there in his eye?—rage, hatred, revenge!

In truth, Rylton's mind is full of evil
thoughts as he strides onward into the
recesses of the wood. The falling autumn
leaves crackle beneath his swift tread, and
through the trees the sky shows signs of
storm. But what storm in all Nature can
be compared with the rage that stirs the
heart of man?

Marian Bethune's covert hints, added to his own suspicions, have set his heart on fire! And that girl's attempts at evasion, her hiding of her brother's faults—all that, too, had been laid bare to him by Marian!

Just now it seems to him as true as life itself that Tita and Tom Hescott have gone for a walk together; somewhere— anywhere beyond the ken of those of her own household. To think that he should have sacrificed his whole life—that he should have married this child, who is less to him than thistledown, to be cast aside by her, and to let her bring down his good name with ignominy to the dust.

He is striding onwards, lost in miserable thought, when suddenly footsteps, coming quickly towards him, rouse him. Some-one is laughing. The laughter strikes to his very soul. When people laugh seldom, one always knows their laugh. Before Tom Hescott turns the corner Rylton knows it is his. But his companion!

'Why, there you are, Rylton!' says

Colonel Neilson at the top of his voice.
' By Jove ! well met ! We've been dis-
puting about a point in the tenant right
down here, and you can set us straight !'

Rylton can hardly account to himself
for the terrible revulsion of feeling he
endures at this moment. Is it joy ? *Can
it be joy ?* What is she to him or he to
her ? Yet positively it is a most thankful
joy he feels as he sees these two men
approaching him together. After all, Minnie
Hescott had been right. It is perhaps
worthy of notice that he does not say to
himself that Marian Bethune had been
wrong !

He sets Colonel Neilson straight on a
point or two, and then goes on again,
striking now, however, into a pathway
that leads him very far from that farm he
had proposed to visit. It opens out into
a pleasant little green sward dotted with
trees, through which the sun glints deli-
cately. One of these trees is a gnarled
old oak

As Rylton steps into this open glade the oak attracts him. He looks at it— first carelessly, and then with sharp in· terest. What strange fruit is that hanging on it ? A foot !—an exquisite little slipper !

He stands still, and looks higher ; and there he sees Tita embedded amongst the leaves, half reclining on a giant bough and reading. The book is on her knees, her eyes upon her book.

CHAPTER XX.

SHE looks like a little elf. All at once the pretty beauty of her breaks upon Rylton. The reaction from such extreme doubt of her to a clear certainty has made his appreciation of her kinder — has, perhaps, opened his eyes to the perfections she possesses. However this may be, there is, beyond question, a great deal of remorse in his soul as he walks towards the tree in which she sits enshrined.

How will she receive him ? Not a word, save those much-begrudged ones at breakfast, has passed between them since last night; and this hurrying away from the others, does it not mean a dislike to meet *him ?*

'You have mounted very high in the world!' says he, stopping beneath the tree and addressing her.

He has come towards her very softly on the grass—so softly that she has not heard his coming. And now, as he speaks, she starts violently, and looks down at him as if surprised out of all measure. In a second, however, she recovers herself.

'True!' says she; 'I have married you!'

It is to be still war, then! Rylton bites his lips, but controls himself. It is plain he is not forgiven. But, after all, she has had something to forgive, and more—*far* more than she even knows. That last suspicion of her was base.

'That is an unkind little speech!' says he gently. 'It reminds me that it was you who set *me* up in the world.'

This shaft tells.

Tita colours warmly ; her generous soul shrinks from such an accusation.

'I didn't mean that,' says she ; 'you know very well I didn't. I wish,' petulantly, 'you would go away ; I want to read.'

'Well, I'm going,' says Rylton. As a means of carrying out this promise, he props himself up with a branch of the tree on which she is sitting—a branch on a level with her dainty little silk-clad feet. He has leant both his arms on it, and now involuntarily his eyes rest upon her shoes. 'What beautiful feet you have !' says he slowly.

It is a perfectly Machiavellian speech. Tita's feet are beyond argument, and there is not a woman in *this* world, any way, who has beautiful feet, who doesn't want every-one to tell her all about them.

'No, no ; they're nothing,' says she, making a pretence of tucking up the much-maligned feet in question under her frock, which basely fails to help her.

But even as she says this she smiles—

reluctantly, no doubt ; but, still, she *does* smile—and casts a glance at Rylton from under her long lashes.   It is a delightful look—half pleased, half defiant, wholly sweet.

‘ Forgive me, Tita !’ says her husband quickly.

‘ I don't want you to talk to me like that,’ says she, with a frown.

‘ But I must say that.   Well, will you ?’

‘ I don't know.’   She stops, and again casts that pretty glance at him.   ‘ At all events, you will have to promise me one thing.’

‘ Anything.’

‘ No ; I'm in earnest.’

‘ So am I.’

He ventures now to take one of the charming feet so close to him into one of his hands, and strokes the instep softly with the other.

‘ Oh no ! you are never in earnest with me,’ says the girl.   ‘ But what I want you to say is, that you won't do it again.’

' Do what ?'

' Scold me.'

' Never—never !' says Rylton.

' That's a promise, mind.'

' I shall mind it.'

' Very well—I forgive you.'

' Let me bring you back to Mother Earth, then,' says Rylton.

' No, thank you ; I can take myself down.'

' That's being unkind to yourself. Take down your friends if you like, but spare yourself.'

' I should like to take *you* down,' says she maliciously.

' Am *I* your friend, then ?'

' No—no, indeed !'

' Well——'

He pauses and looks at her. All at once it seems to him that perhaps he *is* her friend—a friend—a mere friend ! But could a man who loved another woman be an honest friend to his wife ?

' Are you ?' asks Tita.

'Yes. Didn't I want to take you down just now ?'

At this she gives in and laughs a little. He laughs too.

'You are too clever for me,' says she.

'And you—what are you ? Too good for me, perhaps.'

'I don't think you ought to say things you don't mean,' says Tita. 'But as you have made that promise—why, you *may* take me down now.'

She leans towards him, holding out her arms. He takes her into his, and brings her slowly, carefully to the grass beside him. Even when safely landed here he still holds her.

'We *are* friends ?' asks he.

His tone is a question.

'Yes, yes, of course,' impatiently. 'Are they playing tennis ? Do you think they want me ?'

It is impossible for him to misunderstand her meaning. A longing to get back to the others to play, and win at her favourite game of tennis, has been in part the cause of her ready forgiveness.

'Certainly they want you,' says he, surprised at himself for the touch of chagrin he feels. 'But,' still holding her, 'you have quite made it up with me, haven't you ?'

'Quite—quite.'

'But what a way to make it up!' says Rylton reproachfully.

He is smiling all through, however.

'What's the matter with it ?' asks Tita.

'Don't you know ? Must I tell you ? Last night, Tita, you told me you would never want to kiss me again.'

'Well, kissing's a bore,' says Tita, with a little grimace. 'I never want to kiss anyone really, except——'

She hesitates.

'Except ?' asks Rylton, his grasp tighter on her arms.

'Except Margaret.'

Rylton bursts out laughing ; for the moment he believes her, afterwards—

'What a baby you are!' says he; 'and
what a cruel baby! Tita, I shan't believe
you have forgiven me unless you——'

'I think it is *you* who are the baby,'
says she, with a shrug. 'What on earth
do you want to kiss me for? Well, there,'
holding up to him the coolest, freshest
little cheek in the world, 'you can kiss
me if you like.'

'Is that all?' says Rylton, somewhat
piqued.

'Yes—all,' with decision. 'I can't bear
people to kiss me on my mouth.'

'Perhaps you would prefer that people
should not kiss you at all?'

'Well, yes, I should,' says she. 'But,'
quickly, 'of course, you are not quite like
other people. You may kiss my cheek if
you like.'

'Thank you,' says Rylton. 'I appreciate
the difference.'

He kisses her cheek discreetly, but would
have liked to shake her as he does so.

CHAPTER XXI.

EVERYONE has come now, and old Lady
Warbeck, resplendent in pearls and brocade,
has dropped into a chair that some charit-
able person has placed behind her.

It is indeed close upon midnight, and
dancing is at its height. Flowers are
everywhere, and a band from town has
been secured. This latter is quite a flight
on the part of Lady Warbeck, who, as a
rule, trusts the music to the local geniuses.
Altogether everyone acknowledges it is

very well done. Very well done *indeed*,
and a good deal more than one would
expect from the Warbecks !

Old Sir Thomas is marching round,
paying senile compliments to all the
prettiest girls ; his son Gillam, with a
diamond stud that you could see a mile
off, is beaming on Mrs. Bethune, who is
openly encouraging him. Indeed, 'The
Everlasting,' as he is called by his friends
(it is always one's friends who give one a
bad name), is careering round and about
Mrs. Bethune with a vigour hardly to be
expected of him. He is looking even
younger than usual. Though fully forty-
five, he still looks only thirty—the reason
of his nickname ! Everyone is a little surprised at Mrs. Bethune's civility to him,
she having been studiously cold to all men
save her cousin Sir Maurice during the
past year ; but Mrs. Bethune herself is
quite aware of what she is doing. Of
late—it seems difficult of belief—but of
late she has fancied Maurice has avoided

her. He was always a little highflown
with regard to morals, dear Maurice, but
she will reform him! A touch, just a
touch of jealousy will put an end to the
moral question!

She has thrown aside the dark colours
she usually affects, and is to-night all in
white. So is Tita. So is Mrs. Chichester,
for the matter of that. The latter is all
smiles, and is now surrounded by a little
court of admirers at the top of the room,
Captain Marryatt, fatuous as ever, by her
side, and the others encircling her.

'Quite refreshing to see so many men
all together,' says she in a loud voice,
addressing everybody at once. She likes
an audience. 'As a rule, when one gets
into the country, one sticks a glass in one's
eye, and asks, "Where's the MAN?"'

'I never heard anything so unkind in my
life,' says Mr. Gower, with deep reproach.
'I'm sure ever since *you* have been in
the country you have had a regiment
round you, waiting on your lightest word.'

'Oh! you git!' says Mrs. Chichester, who is as vulgar as she is well-born. Her glance roams down the room. 'Just look at Mrs. Bethune and "The Everlasting,"' says she. '*Aren't* they going it? And for once the fair Bethune is well-gowned.'

'Yet I hear she is very hard up at present,' says a woman near her. 'What eyes she has!'

'I was told she made her own gowns,' says another, laughing.

'Pouf!' says Mrs. Chichester. 'That's going a trifle too far. One may make the garment that covers one—I'm sure I don't know, but I've heard it—but no one ever made a *gown* except a regular clothes woman—a modiste.'

'And, for the matter of that, hers is beautiful. Do you see how the catch at the side of the dress is? It shows the bit of satin lining admirably.'

'Well, but how did she get such a charming gown if she is as you say—well, "hard up"?'

'Ah! To go into a thing like that!
How *rude !*' says Mrs. Chichester, going
off into a little convulsion of laughter
behind her fan.

'Talking of clothes,' says Captain Marryatt at the moment, 'did you ever see
anything like Gillam's get up ?'

'Gillam ? Is that Mrs. Bethune's
partner ?'

'Yes. Just look at his trousers, his
diamonds ! How *can* Mrs. Bethune stand
it all ?'

'Perhaps she admires it—the diamonds,
at all events.'

'"My love in his attire doth show his
wit !"' quotes Marryatt, who likes to pose
as a man of letters.

'"When the age is in the wit is out,"'
quotes Gower in his turn, who can never
resist the longing to take the wind out of
somebody's sails; 'and, after all, The
Everlasting is not a youth ! No doubt his
intellect is on the wane.'

'He's a cad, poor fellow !' says one of

the cavalry men from the barracks at
Merriton.

'Nonsense!' says the girl with him, a
tall, heavy creature. 'Why, his father is
a baronet.'

The cavalry man regards her with pity.
How *little* she knows!

'A cad is not always the son of a
sweep,' says he, giving his information
gently; 'sometimes—he is the son of a
prince.'

'Ah! now you are being very funny,'
says the tall girl, who thinks he is trying
to be clever.

'Yes, really, isn't he?' says Mrs.
Chichester, who knows them both; she is
a sort of person who always knows everybody. Give her three days in any neigh-
bourhood whatsoever, and she'll post you
up in all the affairs of the residents there
as well as if she had dwelt amongst them
since the beginning of time. *You*, who
have lived with them for a hundred years,
will be nowhere; she'll always be able to

tell you something about them you never heard before.

'Isn't he?' says she; she is now regarding the heavy girl with suppressed, but keen, amusement. 'And to be funny in this serious age is unpardonable. Don't do it again, Captain Warrender, as you value your life.'

'I shan't!' says he. 'A second attempt might be fatal!'

'How well Mr. Hescott dances!' goes on Mrs. Chichester, who admires Tom Hescott.

'True. The very worst of us, you see, have *one* good point,' says Gower.

'I don't consider Mr. Hescott the worst of you, by a long way,' returns she.

'Oh no, neither do I,' says a pretty little woman next to her, a bride of a few weeks, who, with her husband, has just come up.

'I have you on my side then, Lady Selton?' says Mrs. Chichester.

Lady Selton nods her reply. She is

panting, and fanning herself audibly.
Without the slightest ear for music, she
has been plunging round the room with
her husband, who is still so far infatuated
as to half believe she can dance. She is
an extremely pretty woman, so one can
condone his idiocy.

At this moment Hescott appears. He
goes straight to the bride. He has been
sent, indeed, by Lady Warbeck.

'Will you give me the pleasure of this
dance, Lady Selton?' asks he.

'It? What is it?' nervously.

'A waltz.'

He is smiling at her. She has a charming figure. Of course she can dance.
Tom Hescott would not have asked the
loveliest woman in the land to waltz with
him, if he knew her to be a bad dancer.

'I can't waltz at all,' says the bride.
But her husband comes to the rescue.

'Oh, nonsense!' says he, smilingly.
'Hescott dances so well that he will teach
you. Go, go with him.' He gives her a

playful little push towards Hescott, who is
looking very blank. 'You'll get into it in
no time.'

'Get into it!'

The disgust that is writ so large on
Hescott's face, as he leads her away,
makes Mrs. Chichester shake with
laughter.

'He'll find it a slight difference after
Lady Rylton's waltzing,' says she to
Marryatt.

'He'll find a difference in every way.
Lady Selton is devoted to her husband——'

'And Lady Rylton——'

'*Well?*' He hesitates.

'How vague! But I know, I know!
By-the-bye,' with a swift change of tone
that quite deceives him, 'which do you
admire most?'

'Oh, Lady Rylton, of course. Lady
Selton is pretty—in a way—but——'

'Then you prefer the woman who is *not*
devoted to her husband?'

'I don't see how that argument comes in,' says he quickly. 'Some husbands are —are——'

'Quite true. They are indeed,' interrupts Mrs. Chichester, who seems to be enjoying herself. 'But what an aspersion on poor Sir Maurice.'

'I wasn't thinking of him,' says Marryatt hurriedly.

'Of whom then?'

She fixes her eyes full on his—eyes merry with mischief.

'Oh, I don't know,' says he confusedly.

'Of *my* husband?'

'Mrs. Chichester, I don't think——'

'That's right,' says she, rising and slipping her arm into his. 'Never think; it's about the most foolish thing anyone can do. *I* never think. I only wait; waiting is full of promise.'

CHAPTER XXII.

HOW RYLTON ASKS HIS WIFE TO TREAD A
MEASURE WITH HIM, AND HOW THE
FATES WEAVE A LITTLE MESH FOR TITA'S
PRETTY FEET.

'WILL you give me this dance, Tita?'
asks Sir Maurice, going up to his wife.

Tita is standing in a recess near a
window. The window is wide open, and
filled at each corner with giant ferns in
pots.

'Ye—es,' says Tita, with hesitation.

'Of course, if you are engaged——'

'That's it, I'm not quite sure.'

Rylton laughs unpleasantly.

' Oh, if you want to give it to somebody else——'

' I don't,' returns Tita calmly. ' You
dance better than anyone here, except
Tom.'

' Perhaps, then, you wish to reserve it
for Tom ?   I see you have already danced
a good deal with Tom.'

' It is such a pleasure to dance with
him,' says she enthusiastically.

' One can see how you regard it.'

' What do you mean ?' looking at him.
' Have I danced too much with him ?   If
you imagine——'

' I shouldn't presume to imagine.   But
this dance, why can't I have it ?'

' Well, to tell you the truth, I've lost my
card.   ' I can't think what I have done
with it.'

' Dropped it, perhaps.'

' No ; I *fancy* '—frowning as if trying to
remember—' that I gave it to somebody to
keep for me.'

' Tom, perhaps,' dryly.

'I think not.'

'Well, your partner for this dance, who-
ever he is, doesn't seem to be in a hurry
to claim you,' says Rylton, making his
rude speech very suavely. 'You may as
well give it to me.'

At this moment Hescott, looking rather
out of breath, comes up to them, pushing
the curtain near him aside.

'What a place to hide yourself!' says he
to Tita. 'I have been hunting for you
everywhere.' Here he catches sight of
Rylton. 'Oh, you, Rylton! Tita is in
good company, at all events.'

'She is always in good company, of
course,' returns Rylton, smiling.

'Why, is it *you*, then, who is my
partner?' says Tita, quickly looking at
Tom. 'Maurice wants me to dance this
with him. I told him I should be delighted to, but——'

'Did you tell me that?' interrupts Sir
Maurice, always smiling.

'Well, if I didn't say it, I meant it,'

with a shrug. 'But, you see, I had lost my card, so I wasn't sure whether I was engaged to somebody else or not.'

'Why——' begins Hescott.

He stops dead short. Suddenly it occurs to him that perhaps she doesn't wish her husband to *know!* He curses himself for this thought afterwards. She —*she* to descend to duplicity of any sort!

'It is you who have my card!' cries Tita suddenly, as if just remembering, and with a merry laugh. 'Of course! How could I have forgotten!'

'How, indeed!' says her husband pleasantly; his mouth is looking a little hard, however.

'Give it to me,' says Tita.

Hescott gives her the card in silence. If she is ignorant, he, at all events, is quite aware that there is thunder in the atmosphere.

Tita runs her eye down the card.

'Yes, this dance is yours,' says she, looking up at Tom.

'If you would prefer to dance it with Sir Maurice——' begins he.

He is looking at her. His heart feels on fire. *Will* she elect to dance with this husband, who, as report goes, so openly prefers another?

'No, no, no!' cries Tita gaily; 'I have promised you. Maurice can ask me for another later on.'

'Certainly,' says Sir Maurice courteously.

He nods and smiles at them as they leave the recess, but once past his view, his expression changes; his brow grows black as night. What does it all mean? Is she as innocent as heaven itself, or as false as hell? All things point the latter way.

First she had said—— What was it she had said? That she didn't know whether she were engaged for this dance or not. A clear putting off—a plan to gain time. She had lost her card; she couldn't imagine how or where. Then

comes the inevitable cousin *with* the card.
And his hesitation—that was fatal. He
surely was clever enough to have avoided
that. *She* had known what to do, however ; she had taken the bull by the horns.
She had given ' Tom,' as she calls him, a
safe lead.

And yet—and yet ! Her face comes
back to him. Could he accuse that face
of falsehood ? And another thing : If she
and that cousin of hers were in collusion,
would they have so openly defied him, as
it were ?

No ; it is out of the question. So far
as she goes, at all events, there is nothing
to complain of. That she is indifferent to
him—her husband—is, of course, beyond
question. He himself had arranged all
that beforehand — before his marriage.
Both he and she were to have a loose
rein, and there was to be no call for
affection on either side.

His mind runs back to those early days
when he had asked Tita to marry him.

He had been altogether satisfied with the
arrangements then made — arrangements
that left him as free as air, and his
wife too.   He had thought with boredom
of his marriage, and had grasped at any
alleviation of the martyrdom.   And now
it is just as he had ordained it.   And
yet——

Tita has disappeared.   Once or twice
he had caught a glimpse of her floating
round the room with her cousin, but for
the past five minutes she has not been *en
évidence* at all.   Sir Maurice, moving out
of the recess, is touched by a hand from
behind.   He turns.

Marian Bethune, beautiful, more animated than usual, and with her eyes
sparkling, smiles up at him.

'How dull you look!' cries she gaily.
'Come out here on the balcony and enjoy
the moonlight for awhile.'

She had been standing out there in the
shadow, and had heard and seen what had
occurred between Tita and her husband,

and later on with Tom Hescott. Rylton
follows her. The soft chill of the air outside attracts him. It seems to check all
at once the bitter anger that is raging in
his heart. It surprises himself that he
should be so angry. After all, what is
Tita to him ? A mere name. And
yet——

Outside here the night looks exquisite.
Star after star one sees decking the
heavens with beauty.

> 'Many a night I saw the Pleiads, rising through the
>   mellow shade,
>   Glitter like a swarm of fire-flies tangled in a silver
>   braid.'

Such a night is this, delicate, tender, its
charms heightened by a soft low wind that
sweeps over the gardens and sends a sigh
or two to the balconies above.

'Well !' says Mrs. Bethune.

She has led him to the far end of the
balcony, where no seats are, and where,
therefore, one may be sure of seclusion—
for the moment, at all events. She looks

up at him. Some pale pink lamps from behind throw a slight radiance on her—not too deep a radiance. They are too far behind for that, but yet enough to soften her, to idealize her, and to render even more delicate the exquisite flesh tints of her face.

She has waited for her answer some time, but is well satisfied that no answer has been forthcoming. Rylton's eyes are resting upon hers, as if surprised at this new fairness of hers. His glance is full of admiration, yet there is something of sadness—of anger in it, too, that annoys her, in spite of her exultation. For whom is the anger — for that little fool he has married? It seems to her an absurd thing that he should cast a thought, even an angry one, upon his wife when she — Marian—is here.

She has been leaning upon the rails of the balcony, and now draws closer to him.

'Why waste a thought on her?' says she in a low tone that is almost a whisper.

'On her! Who?' asks he quickly, and with an evident start.

'Oh!' with a shrug. 'If you don't wish to go into it.'

'But into what?'

He frowns. He is feeling very irritable still, in spite of his admiration of her beauty.

She makes a little gesture of contempt.

'If you will not acknowledge me as even your friend.'

'You!' says he sharply. 'You! *Are* you my friend?'

There is a pause. She looks away from him. And then——

'Oh, *more* than that!' cries she in a low but passionate tone. '*Far* more!'

She lays her hand upon her throat, and looks up to heaven. The moonlight, striking upon her as she so stands, makes her fairness even greater.

'Marian! You mean——'

The past rushes in upon him. He has turned to her.

'No! no! It is nothing,' says she, with a little laugh that is full of pain. She makes a movement that almost repulses him. 'But I am your friend, if nothing else ; and the world—the world is beginning to talk about you, Maurice !'

'About me !'

He has drawn back with a sharp pang. She sees that this new idea that touches him, or that little fool (as she has designated Tita in her mind), has destroyed his interest in her for the moment.

'Yes !   Be warned in time.'

'Who is daring to talk about me ?'

'Not about you directly ; but about Lady Rylton.'

Some strange feeling compels him to put a fresh question to her, though he knows what the answer will be.

'My mother ?'

'This is unworthy of you,' says Marian slowly. 'No ; I meant Tita !'

CHAPTER XXIII.

HOW MARIAN FIGHTS FOR MASTERY; AND
HOW THE BATTLE GOES; AND HOW CHANCE
BEFRIENDS THE ENEMY.

'TITA! You wrong her!' says he. 'Why
speak of her? You should not; you
always disliked her.'

'True.' She is silent for a moment,
looking down into the silent garden. Then
she lifts her head, and gazes straight at
him. 'You know why I disliked her. You
must! You—you only. Some instinct
from the very first warned me against her.
I knew. I *knew* she would rob me of all
that life had left me. I knew'—with a
quick, long sob—' she would take *you* from
me!'

Rylton, who has been leaning on the railings beside her, raises himself, and stands staring at her, a terrible anguish in his eyes.

' Marian—think,' says he hoarsely.

' Oh, *why* did you marry her ?' cries she, smiting her hands together as if half distracted. ' There was always so much time —time !'

' There was none.'

' There is always time !' She is silent for a moment, and then, with an increase of passion in her tone, repeats her question : ' Why did you marry her ?'

'*You*—to ask me that !' exclaims he fiercely.

' It was not like you,' says she, interrupting him in a measure, as though unable to keep back the words, the accusations, that are rushing to her lips. ' I have known you so long—so long. Ah ! I thought I knew you. I believed you faithful. I believed you many things. But, at all events '—with a sad and desolate reproach—'I never believed you fond of money.'

'Marian!' She has laid her hand upon his arm, and now he flings it from him. 'That *you* should accuse *me!* Money! What was money to me in comparison with your love? But you—you——'

He does not go on: it is so hard to condemn her. He is looking at her in the tender light with eyes that seek to read her heart, and he is very pale. She can see that, in spite of the warm, pink glow of the lamps behind them.

'Well—and I?' questions she, with deep agitation.

How handsome he is! how lovable! Oh for the good sweet past that she has so madly flung aside!

'You refused me,' says he slowly, 'you, on whom my soul was set.'

'For your own good,' in a stifled voice.

'Don't repeat that wretched formula,' exclaims he vehemently. 'It means nothing. It was not for my good. It was for my damnation, I think. You see how things are going.'

He stops abruptly here, as if thinking of something, and she knows and resents the knowledge that his mind has gone back to Tita—resents it, though his thought has been condemnatory of his wife. Why can't he forget her altogether?

'Yet I meant it for your good,' says she, in a whisper.

Her heart is beating wildly.

'You refused me,' persists he, in a dull tone. 'That is all I remember. You refused me—how many times?'

She turns away from him.

'Once too often, at all events,' replies she, in a low, wretched voice.

She makes a movement as if to go back to the lighted rooms beyond, but he catches her and compels her to stay with him.

'What do you mean?' demands he sternly. 'To say *that* to me—and now—now, when it is too late.'

'Too late, indeed!' echoes she.

Her voice sounds like the voice of one dying. She covers her face with her hands. He knows that she is crying. Very gently he takes down one of the hands and holds it between both his own, and presses it to his lips. How dear she has always been to him! He realizes in this moment how dear she still *is*.

'Marian, have pity on me,' says he hoarsely. 'I have suffered a great deal. And your tears——'

'My tears! They will avail me nothing,' says she bitterly. 'When *you* have forsaken me, what is left?'

'*Have* I forsaken you?' He pauses, as if to control the agitation that is threatening to overcome him. 'When all I cared for was lost to me,' he goes on presently, his eyes upon the ground, 'when you had told me that marriage between us was impossible, then one thing remained, and one only—ambition. The old place had been ours for two centuries—it had its claim on me. If love was not to be my portion, I felt I might as well do all I could for the old name—the old place.'

'And your wife? Was that honourable towards *her?*' She smiles, but her smile is a sneer. 'After all, she would not care,' says she. 'She carried her point! She has compelled you to raise her from the mud to the sky!'

Rylton draws back suddenly. All at once recollection comes to him. His wife! Yes, Tita *is* his wife, and honour binds him to her. He drops Mrs. Bethune's hand.

'I have been quite honourable,' says he coldly. 'I arranged matters with her. She knows—she is content to know—that——'

'What?' Mrs. Bethune has felt the change in his manner ever since she mentioned Tita's name. 'That you once loved me!'

'No,' frowning, 'I have not told her that.'

'Ah!' cries she, with a sort of passionate

relief, ' I thank you for that, even though your love for me may now be dead. I thank you for that ; and as for your wife, what is she to you ?'

' She is my *wife !*' returns he gloomily. ' I shall remember that—always !'

' Ah ! she will *make* you remember it,' cries Marian, with a queer laugh. ' I warn you of *that !*'

' You warn me !'

' Yes—yes.' She throws out her arms in the moonlight, and laughs again, with a great but cruel delight. ' You will see. You don't care for her, she doesn't care for you, and you will see——'

' Marian, take care ! I can hear nothing said against my wife, even by you.'

' You prefer to hear it, then, from others ?' says Mrs. Bethune, leaning back against the railings that overlook the gardens beneath, with a strange smile upon her lips.

' I prefer to believe that there is nothing to hear '—haughtily.

'You can prefer what you like,' says she, with a sudden burst of rage ; 'but hear you shall !'

She takes a step nearer to him.

'I shall not,' says Rylton firmly, if gently. 'She is my wife. I have made her that ! I shall remember it.'

'And she,' says Marian furiously, 'what does *she* remember ? You may forget all old ties, if you will; but she—does *she* forget ?'

'Forget what ?'

Mrs. Bethune laughs softly, sweetly, wildly.

'Are you blind ? Are you *mad ?* Can you see *nothing ?*' cries she, her soft, musical voice now a little harsh and strained. 'That cousin—have you seen nothing there ?'

'You are alluding to Hescott ?'

'Yes—to him, and—Tita !'

'Tita ?' His brow darkens. 'What are you going to say of her ?'

'What you '—deliberately—' do not dare

to say, although you know it—that she is absolutely depraved !'

'*Depraved !*'

'There—stand back !' She laughs, a strange laugh. She has shaken herself free from him. ' Fancy your taking it like that !' says she. She is laughing still, but panting ; the pressure of his hands on her arms is still fresh. ' And have you not seen for yourself, then ? Is it not open to all the world to see ? Is no one talking but *me ?* Why, her flirtation with her cousin is common talk.'

' Depraved, you said !' He has re-covered out of that first wild passion of his, and is now gazing at her with a certain degree of composure. ' Depraved ! I will not have that word used. She is young—thoughtless—foolish, if you will, but not depraved !'

' You can delude yourself just as long as you like,' returns she, shrugging her shoulders, ' but, all the same, I warn you. I——'

She stops suddenly ; voices and steps, coming nearer, check her words. She draws a little away from Rylton, and, lifting her fan, waves it indolently to and fro. The voice belongs to Minnie Hescott, who, with her partner, has come out to the balcony, and now moves down the steps to the lighted gardens below. Mrs. Bethune would have been glad at the thought that Miss Hescott had not seen her ; but there had been one moment when she knew the girl's eyes had penetrated through the dusk where she stood, and had known her.

Not that it mattered much. The Hescott girl was of little consequence at any time. Yet sharp, too ! Perhaps, after all, she *is* of consequence. She has gone, however—and it is a mere question whether she had seen her with Sir Maurice or not. Of course, the girl would be on her brother's side, and if the brother is really in love with that little silly fool—and if a divorce was to be thought of—the girl might make herself troublesome.

Mrs. Bethune, leaning over the railings lost in such thoughts, suddenly sees something.   She raises herself, and peers more keenly into the soft light below.   Yes— yes, *surely !*

But Minnie Hescott, who has gone down the steps into the garden, has seen something too—that fair, fierce face leaning over the balcony !   The eyes are following Tita and her brother, Tom Hescott.

CHAPTER XXIV.

HOW RYLTON MAKES A MOST DISHONOURABLE BET, AND HOW HE REPENTS OF IT ; AND HOW, THOUGH HE WOULD HAVE WITHDRAWN FROM IT, HE FINDS HE CANNOT.

'You have said,' says Rylton, when the steps have ceased, 'that you would warn me about my wife. Of what ?'

She shrugs her shoulders.

'Ah, you are so violent—you take things so very unpleasantly—that one is quite afraid to speak.'

'You mean something'—sternly. 'I apologize to you if I was rough a moment since. I—it was so sudden—I forgot myself, I think.'

' To be able to forget is a most excellent thing—at *times*,' says she, with a curious smile, her eyes hidden. ' If I were you I should cultivate it.'

' It ?'

' The power to forget—*at times !*'

' Speak,' says he. ' It is not a moment for sneers. Of what would you warn me ?'

' I have told you before, but you took it badly.'

' Words—words,' says he, frowning.

'Would you have deeds ?' She breaks into a low laugh. ' Oh, how foolish you are ! Why don't you let things go ?'

' What did you mean ?' persists he icily.

'What a tragic tone !' Her manner is all changed ; she is laughing now. ' Well, what *did* I mean ? That your wife—— Stay !' with a little comic uplifting of her beautiful shoulders and an exaggerated show of fear, ' do not assault me again. That your wife has shown the bad taste to prefer her cousin—her old lover—to you !'

'As I said, words, mere words,' returns he, with a forced smile. 'Because she speaks to him, dances with him, is civil to him, as she is civil to all guests——'

'Is she *just as* civil to all her guests?'

'I think so. It is my part to do her justice,' says he coldly, 'and, I confess, I think her a perfect hostess, if——'

'If?'

'If wanting in a few social matters. As to her cousin, Mr. Hescott—being one of her few relations, she is naturally attentive to him.'

'*Very!*'

'And she is——'

'Always with him!' Mrs. Bethune laughs again — always that low, sweet, cruel laughter. '*Could* attention farther go?'

'Always? Surely that is an exaggeration.'

Rylton speaks with comparative calmness. It is plain that his one outbreak of passion has horrified himself, and he is determined not to give way to another whatever provocation may lie in his path.

'Is it?' tauntingly. 'Come'—gaily—'I will make a bet with you—a fair one, certainly. Of course, I know as little of your wife's movements at present as you do. I could not possibly know more, as I have been here with you all this time.'

'Well—your bet?' darkly.

'That she is now with her old—with Mr. Hescott.'

'I take it,' says he coldly.

Something in his air that is full of anger, of suppressed fury, gives her pause for thought. Her heart sinks. Is she to win or lose in this great game, the game of her life? Why should he look like that, when only the honour of that little upstart is in question?

'Come, then,' says she.

She moves impulsively towards the stairs that lead to the garden—an impulsive step that costs her dear.

'But why this way?' asks Rylton. 'Why

not here ?' pointing towards the ballroom.
' Or *here ?*' contemptuously pointing to a
window further on that leads to a conserva-
tory.

For a moment Mrs. Bethune loses herself—only for a moment, however.   That
first foolish movement that betrayed her
knowledge of where Tita really is has to
be overcome.

' The dance is over,' says she, ' and the
gardens are exquisitely lit.   Lady Warbeck has great taste.   After all, Maurice,'
slipping her hand into his arm, ' our bet is
a purely imaginary one.   We know nothing.
And perhaps I have been a little severe ;
but as it *is* a bet, I am willing to lose it to
you.   Let us take one turn down this
walk that leads to the dahlias, and after
that——'

' After that——'

' Why, *you* win, perhaps.'

' As you will,' says he listlessly.

His heart is still on fire.   Not a word
passes his lips as they go down the path.

His eyes feel strained, hurt; they are
staring—staring always towards the end of
this path, where a seat is, so hedged round
with creepers that one can scarcely see it.
Will she be there? He turns abruptly to
his companion.

' I am sick of this,' says he ; ' I shall go
no farther.'

' But your bet ?'

' It was a damnable bet !' exclaims he
fiercely. ' I ought to be ashamed of myself
for having made it. You win it, of course,
in a sense, as I decline to go on with it ;
but, still, I believe that *I* win it in fact.'

' You are afraid,' says she, with a daring
that astonishes even herself.

' I am afraid of forgetting that once I
was a gentleman,' says he curtly.

' You are afraid of what is in that arbour,'
returns she mercilessly.

Rylton hesitates. To draw back is to
betray disbelief in his wife ; to go on is to
join in a conspiracy against her. He had
started on that conspiracy in a moment of

intense passion, but now his very soul
revolts from it. And yet if he draws back
it will show. . . . It will give this woman
beside him the victory over the woman he
has married. And then a sudden thought
comes to him. Why not go on? Why
not put it to the proof? Why not win his
wager? Tita is thoughtless; but it would
be madness in anyone to think her vile.
It was madness in *him* a moment since to
dream of her being alone in that small,
isolated arbour with Hescott. Much as he
may revolt—as he does revolt—from this
abominable wager he has entered into,
surely it is better to go on with it and bring
it to a satisfactory end for Tita than to
'cry off,' and subject her to scoffs and jeers
from her adversary.

'Let us go on,' says he quietly. ' I shall
win my bet. But that is nothing! What
really matters is, that I should have
entered into such a wager with you or
anyone. That is a debt I shall never be
able to repay—Lady Rylton.'

His tone is bitterly self-condemnatory, but Marian has scarcely caught that. The 'Lady Rylton' has struck upon her ears, and hurt her to her heart's core! Oh, that she could destroy — blot out that small usurper!

'You have regained your courage? Come, then,' says she, in a low tone that is full of a strange mirth.

He follows her along the grassy path— a path noiseless—until presently, having skirted a few low bushes, he finds himself, with Marian beside him, at the southern side of the arbour.

Marian, laying her hand silently upon his arm, points through the evergreens that veil the seat within; a mocking, triumphant smile is on her lips.

There is no need for any indication on her part, however—Rylton can see for himself. On the low, rustic seat within the arbour is Tita—with Hescott beside her. The two young heads are close together. Tita is whispering to Hescott

—something very secret, undoubtedly. Her small face is upturned to his, and very earnest. *His* face.

Rylton never forgets his face !

Tita is speaking—she is smiling—she leans toward her companion ; her voice is full of a delicious confidence.

'Well, remember it is a secret—a secret between us.'

Rylton draws back as if stabbed. He would have given his soul to hear the end of this terrible beginning—this beginning that, at all events, sounds so terrible to *him ;* but the fact that he *is* longing to hear, that he has been listening, makes him cold from head to heel.

He moves away silently. Mrs. Bethune, catching his arm, says quickly :

'You heard—a secret—a secret between those two—you *heard !*'

There is something delirious in her tone —something that speaks of revenge perfected, that through all his agitation is understood by him. He flings her hand

aside, and goes swiftly onwards alone into
the dense darkness of the trees beyond,
damning himself as he goes. A very rage
of hatred, of horror of his own conduct, is
the first misery that assails him, and after
that——

After that he sees only Tita sitting there
with Hescott beside her—he whispering to
her, and she to him.

He stops in his rapid walk, and pulls
himself together : he must have time—
time to think, to control himself, to work it
all out.

Things seem to come back to him with
a strange clearness. He remembers how
Tita had once said to him that she never
cared to kiss anyone except—Margaret.
His hesitation returns to him now ; was
Margaret the name she would have said
had not fear, mixed with prudence,
prompted her words ? He remembers,
too, that she had once refused to let *him*
kiss her lips—him, her husband ! Why ?
He trembles with rage as he asks himself

this question.   Was it to keep them sacred
for someone else—for that 'old lover' of
hers, for example?

Who had called him that?   Marian, was
it not?   Old lover!

He had laughed at the name then.   That
child to have a lover!   Why, he had
believed she did not know the meaning
of the word 'love.'   What a baby she had
always seemed to him—a careless, troublesome baby.   And now!

Great heavens!   Who is to be trusted?
Is anyone to be trusted?   He had put his
faith in Tita; he had thought her wild,
perhaps a little unmanageable, but—yes, he
had thought her lovable; there had been
moments when——

And now it had all come to this, that
she had deceived him—is wilfully deceiving
him.

He does not even in this, his angry
hour, accuse her of more than a well-
developed flirtation with her cousin; but
that is the beginning of an end that he will

put a stop to at once, and for ever. He
will show her who is her master. If she
cannot respect herself, he will, at all events,
take care that she respects his name ; she
shall not disgrace *that*.

He has hardly known where his feet
have taken him, but now he finds himself
on a lighted path, with two or three couples
coming towards him ; evidently they have
just left the dancing-room. He has therefore described a circle, and come back to
the place from which he started. One
of the men passing him looks into his
face.

That quick, curious glance brings Rylton
to himself. He cannot stay here any
longer. He must go back to the house.
It will be madness to absent himself. And,
after all, is not the whole thing madness ?
What is this girl to him ? A mere name ;
nothing more.

He mounts the steps leading to the con-
servatory, and, meeting Minnie Hescott,
asks her to dance.

' This is only a supper dance,' says she. ' I'm engaged for all the rest. But, if you like, I'll take one turn with you. After that you must get me something to eat ; I never felt so hungry in all my life.'

CHAPTER XXV.

HOW TITA TOLD A SECRET TO TOM HESCOTT IN THE MOONLIGHT; AND HOW HE SOUGHT TO DISCOVER MANY THINGS, AND HOW HE WAS MOST INNOCENTLY BAFFLED.

'OF course, I shall understand that it is a secret,' says Tom Hescott.

Both he and Tita are quite unaware of the fact that Rylton and Mrs. Bethune had just been standing behind them. Tita, who had been dancing with Hescott, had led the way to this spot when they came out into the garden.

'Still,' says Tita, hesitating, 'perhaps I ought not to speak. A secret *is* a secret, you know.'

'Yes; everyone knows that,' says Hescott.

'Knows what?' sharply.

'About a secret.'

'If you're going to be nasty, you shan't know it at all,' says Tita. 'I understand you very well. You think no woman can keep a secret.'

'Ah! but a man can. Tell me yours.'

'Nonsense! A woman is *twice* as good at keeping a secret as a man is. And I can tell you this'—with a little emphatic shake of her charming head — 'that I should not tell *you* anything of this secret, only that you are always calling her names.'

'Her? Who?'

'Oh, you know very well.'

'Who do I know very well? Not a soul here except you; and, after all, I don't think I know *you* very well.'

'Well, if you don't you ought.'

'Ought what? Know the mysterious "her" or you?'

' *Me !*'

Hescott looks at her keenly in the dim light. *Is* she a born coquette, or is she only a sweet child—the sweetest child that ever earth gave forth ? Somehow it would have hurt him to find her a coquette.

' Ah ! I *don't* know you.'

' Tom !' There is a little reproach in her tone. Suddenly she puts out her little slim hand and slips it into his. ' As if we weren't brought up together,' says she, ' just like a brother and sister. You remember the old days, don't you, Tom ? when we used to go fishing together, and the cricket——'

' Is it wise to remember ?' says Hescott in a low tone.

His heart is beating ; his fingers now close on hers.

' I don't know—yes. Yes, I think I like to,' says Tita. ' Darling pappy ! Sometimes it all comes back to me. How happy I was then !'

'And now, Tita, *now!*—are you happy now?' asks he.

His tone is almost violent. The pressure of his hand on hers grows hurtful. Involuntarily she gives a little cry.

'Nonsense! Of course I am happy!' says she petulantly, pulling her hand out of his. 'How rough you are, Tom!'

'Did I hurt you?' exclaims he passionately. 'Tita, forgive me. To hurt you——'

'There, don't be a fool!' says Tita, laughing. 'My fingers are not broken, if that's what you mean. But you certainly *are* rough: and, after all' — mischievously—'I don't think I shall tell you that secret now.'

'You must. I shan't sleep if I don't know it. You said I knew the heroine of it.'

'Yes, you do indeed,' laughing.

'And that I was always calling her names?'

'True; and I can't bear that, because'

—gently—' I love her.' She pauses, and goes on again very earnestly : ' I love her with all my heart.'

' I envy her,' says Hescott. ' I'm glad this mysterious stranger is a she.'

' Why ?'

' Oh, no matter ; go on.   Tell me more. What evil names have I called her ?'

' The worst of all.   You have called her an old maid—there !'

' Good heavens!   what an   atrocity ! Surely—surely you malign me.'

' No, I don't ; I heard you.   And it was to me, too, you said it.'

' What ! I called you an old maid !'

' Pouf!   No !' laughing gaily.   ' That's out of your power.'

' It is indeed,' says Hescott slowly.

He is looking at her, the little, pretty, sweet, lovely thing ! If she were a maid to-day, some chance—some small chance —might have been his.

' Well, I'll tell you about it,' says she. She looks round her cautiously, in the

funniest little way, as if expecting enemies
in the bushes near her. Then she hesitates. 'After all, I won't,' says she, with
the most delightful inconsistency.   It
wouldn't be a secret if I did.'

'Oh, go on,' says Hescott, seeing she is
dying to speak. 'A secret told to me is
as lost as though you had dropped it down
a well.'

'You must remember first, then, that I
should never have told you, only that you
seemed to think she *couldn't* get married.
It'—hesitating—'it's about Margaret!'

'Miss Knollys!' Hescott stares. 'What
has she been up to?'

'She has been refusing Colonel Neilson
for *years!*' solemnly.   'Only this very
night she has refused him again ; and all
because of a silly old attachment to a man
she knew when she was quite a girl.'

'That must have been some time ago,'
says Hescott irreverently and unwisely.

'A very *few* years ago,' severely.   She
rises.   She is evidently disgusted with

him. 'Come back to the house,' says she.
'I am engaged for the next.'

'A word,' says Tom, rising and following her. He lays a detaining hand upon
her soft, little, bare arm. 'You blame her
—Miss Knollys—for being faithful to an
old attachment?'

'Y-es,' says Tita slowly, as if thinking,
and then again, 'Yes!' with decision.
'When the old attachment if of no use any
longer, and when there is someone else.'

'But if there was an old attachment,
and'—Hescott's face is a little pale in the
moonlight—'and practically—no one else
—how then?'

'Eh?'

'I mean, if'—he comes closer to her—
'Tita, if *you* had known a man who loved
you before you were married, and if when
you did marry——'

'But she didn't marry him at all,' interrupts Tita. 'He died—or something—I
forget what.'

'Yes; but think.'

'There is nothing to think about. He died—so *stupid* of him ; and now she is making one of the nicest men I know miserable, all because she has made up her mind to be wretched for ever ! So stupid of *her !*'

'Has it ever occurred to you that there is such a thing as love ?' asks Hescott, looking at her with a sudden frown.

'Oh, I've heard of it,' with a little light shrug of her pretty shoulders ; 'but I don't believe in it. It's a myth ! a fable !'

'And yet'—with an anger that he can hardly hide, seeing her standing there so young, so fair, so debonnair before him— so insensible to the passion for her that is stirring within his heart—'and yet your friend, Miss Knollys, is giving up her life, you say, to the consecration of this myth.'

Tita nods.

'Yes ; isn't she silly ? I *told* you she was very foolish.'

'You assure me honestly that you don't believe in love ?'

'Not a bit,' says Tita. 'It's all nonsense! Now come in—I want to dance.
And remember — remember, Tom, you
have promised not to breathe a word about
what I have told you.'

'I promise,' says Hescott in a slow sort
of way; he is thinking.

When they reach the dancing-room they
find it, comparatively speaking, empty,
save for a few enthusiastic couples who are
still careering round it.

'Supper must be on,' says Hescott.
'Come and have something.'

*   *   *   *   *

As they enter the supper-room several
people look at them. To Rylton, who is
standing near Mrs. Bethune, these glances
seem full of impertinent inquiry. In
reality they mean nothing, except admiration of his wife. To-night Lady Rylton
has been pronounced by most of those.
present the prettiest woman in the room.
Hescott pilots his charming companion to
a low lounge in a corner of the room, a

place at any of the tables being impossible
to get. But Rylton decides that he has
taken her to that secluded spot to make
more conspicuous his flirtation with her ;
and she—she seems only too ready to help
him in his plan.

The fact that he is frowning heavily is
conveyed to him by a voice at his elbow.

'*Don't* look so intense — so like a
thirteenth-century conspirator !' says Mrs.
Bethune.   Her eyes are full of laughter
and mischief — there is something of
triumph in them too.   'What does it
matter, after all ?'

'True.'   He gives her a brilliant smile
in return for her rather mocking one.
'Nothing matters — except the present
moment.   Let us consider it.   Are you
engaged for this dance ?'

'Yes; but I can manage to forget my
partner.'

'That means ?'

'You know very well what it means—
what it always meant—in the old days.'

Her lips part over her beautiful teeth ; now there is no mockery in her smile, only love, and a most exquisite delight.

'Ah, Marian !' says he, in a low tone.

He leads her from the room. Her hand tightens on his arm ; he feels the pressure, and now in the ball-room his arm goes round her. She—the woman he had loved for so long—is in his arms ; he forgets everything. He has sworn to himself in the last minute or two that he *will* forget. Why, indeed, should he re-member ?

For the rest of the evening he gives himself up to Marian—devoting himself to her ; telling himself he is knowing the old sweet happiness again, but always with a strange unaccountable sting at his heart.

CHAPTER XXVI.

HOW TITA LOOKS AT HERSELF IN THE GLASS, AND WONDERS; AND HOW SHE DOES HER HAIR IN QUITE A NEW STYLE, AND GOES TO ASK SIR MAURICE WHAT HE THINKS OF IT; AND HOW HE ANSWERS HER.

'You can go to bed, Sarah; I shan't want you. And any other night when I am out so late you must not stop up for me. Do you hear?'

'Oh! But, my lady——'

'Yes, yes, yes; I know,' interrupting her gaily. 'But I won't have it. Do you think I can't take off my own frocks? You will lose your beauty sleep, and I shall be responsible for it. There, go; I'm all right now.'

Tita waves her gaily out of the room. She is indeed in the merriest mood, having enjoyed her evening immensely, and danced to the very last minute. She had been thoroughly sorry when Sir Maurice had told her that she ought to say 'Good-night' to her hostess and come home. She had not noticed the coldness of his manner at all, being so disappointed at his suggestion; but she had said 'Good-night' at once to old Lady Warbeck, who would have liked her to stay on, having taken a great fancy to her; and as she had come back in a brougham with Margaret and Colonel Neilson and Minnie Hescott, she had not seen her husband since.

Having at last dismissed her maid, who had insisted on waiting to take off her evening dress, Tita sits down before the glass to look at herself (all women like looking at themselves), and to think over her evening.

How well the men danced, especially Tom!—though, after all, not so well as

Maurice. What a pity she could not have had that *one* dance with him he had asked her for.

She leans forward, and pulling some hairpins out of her short, curly hair, pushes it into another shape, a little lower down on the neck, to see if that would suit her better. No, it wouldn't.

After all, Maurice *might* have asked her again. He danced a great deal with Mrs Bethune towards the end of the evening, and how charming he looked when dancing!

She rests her arms—soft, naked arms, round and white as a child's—upon the dressing-table and wonders. Wonders if that old story—the story her mother-in-law had told her of Maurice and Mrs. Bethune—was really true. Maurice did not look like that—like a man who would be dishonest. Oh no! It is not true—that horrid story!

Her eyes light up again ; she goes back again to her hair, the arrangement of which, on account of its length, is difficult.

She piles it now far up on her head, and sticks little diamond pins into it. She almost laughs aloud. She looks like a Japanese young woman. And it's very pretty, too—she *does* look nice in this way. What a pity nobody can see her! And with this little new white dressing-gown, too! Such a little dream of a thing !

Where's Maurice ? Surely he must have come up by this time. Some of the men had gone into the smoking-room on their return ; but it is so late—with the dawn breaking ; perhaps Maurice *has* come up.

She crosses a little passage and goes to the door leading into his room, and knocks lightly ; no answer. She knocks again, more impatiently this time, and as still only silence follows her attempt, she opens the door and steps on tiptoe into the room.

It is lit by two or more lamps, and at the end of it, close to a hanging curtain, stands Maurice in his trousers and shirt, having evidently just flung off his evening coat.

'Oh, here you are!' cries she with open delight. 'I was afraid you hadn't come up yet, and I wanted to show myself to you. Look at my hair!' She pulls out the skirts of her dainty loose gown and dances merrily up to him. 'Don't I look lovely?' cries she, laughing.

Rylton has turned; he is looking at her; his eyes seem to devour her—more with anger than delight, however. And yet the beauty of her, in spite of him, enters into his heart. How sweet she is, standing there with her loose gown in her pretty uplifted hands, and the lace flounces of her petticoat showing in front! She had not fastened this new delight in robes across her neck, and now the whiteness of her throat and neck vies with the purity of the gown itself.

> 'He looked on her and found her fair,
> For all he had been told.'

Yet a very rage of anger against her still grows within his heart.

'What brought you here?' asks he sharply, brutally.

She drops her pretty gown. She looks at him as if astonished.

'Why—because'—she is moving backwards towards the door, her large eyes fixed on him—'because I wanted you to look at me—to see how nice I am.'

'Others have looked too,' says he. 'There, go. Do you think I am a fool?'

At that Tita's old spirit returns to her. She stands still and gives him a quick glance.

'Well, I never thought so till now,' says she. She nods at him. 'Good-night.'

'No, stop!' says Rylton. 'I will have this out with you. You pretend to misunderstand me; but I shall make it clear. Do you think I have not seen your conduct of this evening?'

'Mine?'

'Yes, with your cousin—with Hescott.'

He draws nearer to her. His eyes are on fire, his face white. ' Do you think I saw nothing ?'

' I don't know what you saw,' says she slowly.

All her lovely mirth has died away, as if killed by a cruel death.

' Don't you ?' tauntingly. ' Then I will tell you. I saw you '—he pauses as if to watch the changes of her face, to see when fear arises, but none does—' in the arbour ' —he pauses again, but again no fear arises —' with your cousin.'

He grows silent, studying her with eager eyes, as if expecting something ; but nothing comes of all his scrutiny, except surprise. Surprise, indeed, marks all her charming features.

' Well ?' says she, as he stops, as if expecting more.

She waits, indeed, as one at a loss.

' Well ?' He repeats the word with a wild mockery. Could there be under heaven another woman so dead to all

honesty ?   Does she dare to think she can
deceive him to the end ?   In what a lovely
form the devil can dwell !   ' Well !'   He
brings down his hand with a little crash
upon the table near her.   ' I was there—
near that arbour.   I heard—I heard all.'

' Well, I'm sorry,' says Tita slowly,
colouring faintly.

' Sorry !   Is that all ?   Do you know
what it means—what I can do ?'

' I don't see that you can do anything,'
says she, thinking of her revelation to
Hescott about Margaret.   ' It is Colonel
Neilson who might do something.'

' Neilson ?'

'Yes, Colonel Neilson.'

' Are you mad ?' says Sir Maurice, in a
low tone, ' to think you can thus deceive
me over and over again ?'

He draws back from her.   Disgust is in
his heart.   Does she dream that she can
pass off Neilson as her lover, instead of
Hescott ?   He draws a sharp breath.   How
she must love Hescott, to seek thus to

shield him, when ruin is waiting for herself!

'I am not mad,' says Tita, throwing up
her head. 'And as to deceiving you——
Of course I can see that you are very
angry with me for betraying Margaret's
secret to Tom; but, then, Tom is a great
friend, and when he said something about
Margaret's being an old maid, I couldn't
bear it any longer. You *know* how I love
Margaret!—and I told him all about
Colonel Neilson's love for her, and that
she *needn't* be an old maid unless she
liked. But as to deceiving you——'

Rylton, standing staring at her, feels
that it is the truth—the truth only—to
which he is listening. Not for a moment
does he disbelieve her. Who could, gazing
on that small, earnest face? And yet his
silence breathes of disbelief to her. She
steps backwards, and raises her little hand
—a little hand very tightly clenched.

'What! Do you not believe me?' asks
she, her eyes blazing.

'I believe you? Yes,' returns he quickly. 'But there is this——'

'There is this, too,' interrupting him passionately. 'You accuse me of deception most wrongfully, and I—I accuse you of the worst thing of all, of listening behind my back—of listening deliberately to what was never meant for you to hear.'

'I did not listen,' says Rylton, who is now very white. 'It so chanced that I stood near the arbour; but I heard only one word, and it was about some secret. I came away then. I did not stay.'

Tita turns to him with a vehemence that arrests him.

'Who brought you to the arbour?' asks she.

'Brought me?'

'Yes. Who brought you?'

'What do you mean?' asks Rylton, calmly enough, but with a change of colour.

'Ah! you will not betray her, but I know. It was Mrs. Bethune. Now'— she goes nearer to him, her pretty, childish

face transformed by grief and anger—
'now, confess; it *was*!' She draws back
again. 'No,' says she, sighing discon-
solately. 'No, of course you would not
tell. But I,' looking back at him reproachfully, '*I*—told *you*—things.'

'Many things,' returns he coldly—un-
reasonably angry with her because of her
allusion to Mrs. Bethune; 'and hardly to
your credit. Why should you tell Mr.
Hescott your secrets? Why is he to be
your confidant?'

'I have known Tom all my life.'

'Nevertheless, I object to him as a
special friend for you. I don't think
married women should have special friends
of the other sex. I object to your con-
fiding in him secrets that you never told
to me. You said nothing to me of Margaret's love affairs, although she is my
cousin.'

'You forget, Maurice. I spoke to you
several times, but you never seemed to
care. And I should not have told Tom,

only he called her an old maid, and that
hurt me, and I wanted to show him how
it was. I love Margaret, and I—I am
fond of Tom, and——'

The hesitation, though unmeant, is fatal.
Rylton turns upon her furiously.

'It is of no consequence to me whom
you love or whom you—*care* for,' says he,
imitating her hesitation, with a sneer.
'What *is* of consequence to me, is your
conduct as my wife, and that I object to
altogether !'

There is a long pause, and then—

'*My* conduct ?' says she slowly. She
lifts her hands and runs them softly through
her loose hair, and looks at him all the
time ; so standing, few could vie with her
in beauty. She pauses. 'And yours ?'
asks she.

'Mine ?'

'Yes, yours ! I don't know what you
mean about my conduct. But you, you
have been dancing all the night with that
horrid Mrs. Bethune. Yes !'—letting her

hands fall, and coming towards him with a face like a little angry angel—'you may say what you like, but you *have* been dancing all night with her. And she *is* horrid.'

This is carrying the war into the enemy's camp with a vengeance. There is something in her tone that startles Rylton. Has she heard of that old attachment? His heart grows sick within him. Has it come to this, then? Is there to be concealment—deception on *his* part? Before his marriage he had thought nothing of his love for Marian in so far as it could touch his wife, but now—now, if she knows! But how can she know? And besides——

Here his wrath grows warm again. Even if she does know, how does that affect her own behaviour? Her sin is of her own making. *His* sin—— Was it ever a sin? Was it not a true, a loyal love? And when hope of its fulfilment was denied him, when he placed a barrier

between it and him, had he not been true
to that barrier ?   Only to-night—to night
when, maddened by the folly of this girl
before him — he had let his heart stir
again—had given way to the love that
had swayed him for two long years and
more.

'You forget yourself,' says he coldly.

'Oh no, I don't,' says Tita, to whom
this answer sounds rather overbearing.
'Why should I ?'   She glances at him
mischievously from under her long lashes.
'I should be the most unselfish person
alive if I did that.'   She hesitates for a
moment, and then, 'Do you ever forget
yourself ?' asks she saucily.

She laughs—her little saucy air suits her.
She is delighted with herself for having
called Mrs. Bethune 'horrid,' and given him
such a delicious tit-for-tat.   She looks full
of fun and mischief.   There is no longer
an atom of rancour about her.   Rylton, in
spite of himself, acknowledges her charm ;
but what does she mean by this sudden

sweetness—this sudden sauciness? Is she holding out the olive-branch to him? If so, he will accept it. After all, he may have wronged her in many ways; and at all events, her faults—her very worst fault —must fall short of crime.

'Sometimes,' replies he. He smiles. 'I forgot myself just now, perhaps. But you must admit I had provocation. You——'

'Oh, don't begin it all over again,' cries she, with delightful *verve*. 'Why should you scold me, or I scold you? Scolding is very nasty, like medicine.' She makes a little face. 'And, you know, before we married we arranged everything.'

'Before?'

'Yes, before, of. course. Well—good-night!'

'No; don't go. Tell me what it was we arranged before our marriage?'

Rylton has drawn a chair for her towards the fire that is lighting in his grate, and now sinks into another.

' It's awfully late, isn't it ?' says Tita, with a yawn, 'but I'll stay a minute or two. Why, what we arranged was, that we should be good friends, you and I— eh ?'

' Well ?'

' Well—that's all. Poke up the fire, and let me see a blaze. Fancy your having a fire so early !'

' Haven't you one ?'

' Yes. But then I'm a woman. However, when I see one I want it poked. I want it blazing.'

At this Sir Maurice pokes the fire, until it flames well up the chimney.

' Ah ! I like that,' says Tita. She slips from her chair to the hearthrug—a beautiful white soft Persian one—and sits upon it, as it were, one snowflake on another. ' How nice it is !' says she, staring at the sparks roaring up the chimney ; 'such a companion !' She leans back and rests her head against Rylton's knees. ' Now, go on,' she says comfortably.

'Go on?'

'Yes.   We were saying something about friends.   That *we* should be friends all our lives.   So we shall be.   Eh?'

'I don't know.'   Rylton bends over her, and, suddenly laying his hand under her chin, lifts her face so that he can see it.   'You mean that I shall be your friend, and you mine.'

'Yes.   Yes, of course.'

'You have other friends, however.   And I don't like that.'

'What!   Is one to have only one friend?'   She wriggles her face out of his hands, and moving her body as she reclines upon the white rug, so turns herself that she comes face to face with him. 'Only one!' says she, smiling.   She flings her arms across his knees, and looks up at him.

'Is not one enough?'   He is looking at her very earnestly.   How lovely she is!   What a strange charm lies in her deep eyes!   And her smile—

'The smile that rests to play
Upon her lip, foretells
That musical array
Tricks her sweet syllables.'

'Oh, it would be a poor world with only one friend,' says she, shaking her head.

'You want two?' His brow is darkening again.

'More than that. I want you, and Margaret, and——'

'Hescott?'

It is not so much that she has hesitated as that he has not given her time to speak.

'Well, yes—Tom,' says she. 'He *is* my friend!'

'The best of all?' She is not looking at him now, so does not see the expression in his eyes. He is listening breathlessly for her answer, but she knows nothing. She is gazing idly, happily, into the fire.

'At present,' says she slowly. Then once again she leans across his knees, and looks up at him. 'You know Tom is very fond of me—he loves me, I think.'

Here Rylton lays his hands upon her wrists, grasping them hard. .

'He loves you. He has told you so?'

'No. Why should he?' He lets her hands go. 'I know it. He has loved me so many years ; and perhaps—in many years'—she comes closer to him, and putting up one soft little hand, lays it on his cheek, and tries to turn his face to hers —'*you* will love me too!'

Sir Maurice springs to his feet, and, catching her hands, lifts her forcibly to hers.

'There, go,' says he, as if choking. 'Is that how you speak to *him* ?'

'To him ?'

She stands back from him—not trembling, but with a terrible wonder in her eyes.

'To Hescott—— There—go.'

'You think——' says she.

'I think you what you are, a finished

coquette.' He almost pushes her from him.

Tita puts up her hands as if to warn him off.

'I am sorry I ever came here,' says she at last. 'I am sorry I ever married you. I shall never forgive this—never!'

'And I,' says Rylton. 'Have *I* nothing to forgive?'

'Nothing, nothing,' passionately. 'I came here to-night because I was lonely, and wanted to talk to somebody. I came here to show you my pretty new frock; and how have you received me? You have been *hateful* to me. And yet you wonder that I don't think you my best friend! You are not a friend at all. You can't bear me! If I had gone to Tom, instead of you—to show *him* my frock— do you think he would have treated me like this? No, he——'

'Be silent!' says Sir Maurice. 'How *dare* you talk to me like this!' A dark flush has risen to his brow, his nostrils are dilated. Is she mad—to say such things to him? 'Go!' says he, pointing imperiously to the door.

'You have said that twice!' returns she in a low tone. A moment her eyes rest on his, in another moment she is gone.

All that is left him is the memory of a little lovely creature, clad in a white gown, who had come to him with merry, happy eyes, and a smile upon her lips—a smile that he had killed!

CHAPTER XXVII.

HOW SIR MAURICE FEELS UNEASY; AND HOW TITA, FOR ONCE, SHOWS HERSELF IMPLACABLE, AND REFUSES TO ACCEPT THE OVERTURES OF PEACE. AND HOW A LITTLE GOSSIP WARMS THE AIR.

IT is the next day, and luncheon is well over, a somewhat badly-attended meal. But now all have managed to scramble downstairs, and the terrace is full of people who are saying 'Good-morning' to each other at four o'clock in the afternoon.

'I never felt so tired in my life,' says Mrs. Chichester, subsiding into a lounging chair, and trying to look as if her tea-gown isn't quite new. She has selected this evening in especial to spring it upon

her women friends.   As a rule people
look dowdy after being up all night.   Mrs.
Chichester is determined *she* won't.   She
appears as fresh as the proverbial lark, in
an exquisite arrangement of white silk
and lace, and a heavenly temper.   Her
eyes are a little greener than usual.

'You don't look it,' says Sir Maurice,
who is standing near.   He is wondering
if Tita will come down.   Tita has not
put in an appearance all day.   There had
been no necessity to send an apology
about her absence from breakfast, as
almost every one of the women had taken
that meal in her own room, but she *had*
sent a word or two of regret about her
inability to appear at luncheon, and, somehow, it has got into Sir Maurice's mind
that perhaps she has made up her mind
to stay in her own rooms all day.   The
thought makes him uneasy ; but at this
moment an end is put to it.

There is a little stir on his left, and,
looking up, he sees Tita coming towards

him down the terrace, stopping at every
step to say a word to somebody. Now
she stops as she comes to Margaret, and,
laying her hands upon her shoulders, kisses
her. She is dressed in the simplest little
white frock in the world—a frock that
makes her look even younger than usual.
Her pretty short hair is curling all over
her head, and her dark gray eyes are *very*
dark to-day. Do shadows lie in them, or
has she been crying? It is Rylton who,
watching her, asks himself this question,
and as he asks it a strange pang shoots
through his heart. Good heavens! why
had he married her? To make her
unhappy? He must have been possessed
of the devil when he did that deed.

'How pretty you look, Tita!' Margaret
whispers to her—Margaret, who has the
gift of knowing how to soothe and please.
She, too, has her misgivings about those
lovely eyes; but all girls like to be told
that they are pretty, and Tita at once
brightens.

'Am I? You are a goose, Madge!'
But she presses Margaret's hands fondly
for all that as she leaves her.

'Lady Rylton, come and sit here,' cries
Mrs. Chichester. 'I have a lovely chair
here for you. It's as soft as——' She
cannot find a simile.

'As what?' asks Gower, who delights
in annoying Mrs. Chichester.

'As you!' returns she, with a contemptuous glance that fills him with joy.

'Come,' says Mrs., Chichester, calling
again to Tita, and patting the chair in
question. 'You look tired. This is a
perfect lounge.'

'She looks as if she had been crying,'
says old Miss Gower, frowning at Tita
over her glasses.

Again that strange pang contracts
Rylton's heart. *Has* she been crying—
and because of him?

'Looks! What are looks?' cries Mrs.
Chichester gaily. 'Looks always belie
one.'

'Certainly Lady Rylton's must belie *her*,' says Mrs. Bethune, with a slow smile. 'What cause has she for tears?'

'Not one!' declares Mrs. Chichester with decision. 'It would be "a sinner above all the Galileans" who would make Lady Rylton cry.'

Her queer green eyes smile at Tita, who smiles back at her in her little sweet way, and then all at once bursts out laughing. It is a charming laugh, apparently full of mirth. There are only two present who do not quite believe in it, Margaret and Tom Hescott—but these two love her.

As for Rylton, some instinct causes him at this moment to look at Hescott. Tita's cousin is staring at her, his brows met, his lips somewhat compressed. He has forgotten that people may be staring at him in return, maybe measuring his thoughts on this or that. He has forgotten everything, indeed, except Tita's pale, laughing face and dancing, tear-stained eyes.

'Do you see a ghost?' whispers Mrs.
Bethune to him, who has been watching
him with cruel amusement.

' I don't know,' he answers, hardly hearing her.   Is not Tita to-day a ghost of
her sweet self?   And those words, 'A
sinner   above   all   the   Galileans!'   *Is*
there such a sinner?—and if so, surely
it is——

Hescott lifts his eyes to meet those of
Rylton.   For a moment the two men
regard each other steadily, and in that
moment know that each hates the other
with an undying intensity.   Mrs. Bethune,
who alone sees the working of the little
tragedy, leans back in her chair, and lets
her lids fall over her eyes.   So still she
lies that one might think her sleeping, but
she is only battling with a fierce joy that
threatens every moment to break its
bonds, and declare her secret to the
world !

During all this, conversation has been
going on.   Last night's sayings and doings

are on the *tapis*, and everyone is giving
his and her experiences. Just now the
rather disreputable wife of a decidedly
disreputable neighbour is lying on the
social dissecting board.

'She gives herself away a good deal, I
must say,' says Mrs. Chichester, who
loves to hear her own voice, and who
certainly cannot be called ungenerous on
her own account. 'The way she dances!
And her frock! Good heavens!'

'I hear she makes all her own clothes,'
says Margaret, who perhaps hopes that
this may be one small point in her favour.

Minnie Hescott makes a little *moue*.

'She may possibly make the things
that cover her——'

'That *what?*' questions Mr. Gower,
resting innocent eyes on hers, but Miss
Hescott very properly refuses to hear
him.

'It must be a matter for regret to all
well-minded people,' says Miss Gower,
shaking her head until all her ringlets

are set flying, 'that when making that hideous dress, she did not add a yard or two, to——' She pauses.

'The what?' asks Mrs. Chichester, leaning forward.

'The *bodice!*' replies Miss Gower severely.

'Oh, auntie!' says her nephew, falling back in his chair and covering his face with his hands. 'You shouldn't! You really shouldn't! It's—it's not delicate!'

'What do you mean, Randal?' demands his aunt, with a snort that would have done credit to a war-horse. 'To whom are you addressing your remarks? Are you calling *me* indelicate?'

'Oh no—not for worlds!' says Mrs. Chichester, who is choking with laughter, and who only emerges from behind her fan to say this, and go back again. 'Who could? But we feared—we thought you were going to say her *skirt.*'

'It is my opinion that you fear nothing,' says Miss Gower, with a withering glance at the fan. 'And let me tell you that there are *other* people'—with awful emphasis—'besides Mrs. Tyneway who would do well to put a tucker round their——'

'Ankles!' puts in Mrs. Chichester sweetly.

'No; their——'

'What was her dress made of?' breaks in Margaret hurriedly, who is afraid of their going too far with the irascible old lady.

'Goodness knows! She was all black and blue, at all events!'

'No! You don't say so?' exclaims Mr. Gower, with a tragic gesture. 'So her husband has been at it again!'

At this they all roar, as people will, at *anything*, when they have nothing else to do. Even Tita, who, though smiling always, is looking rather depressed, gives way to a merry little laugh. Hearing her, Margaret blesses Randal for his silly old joke.

'Oh, Randal!' you are too stupid for

anything,' says Tita, showing all her pretty teeth.

'You have for once lighted on a solemn truth,' puts in Randal's aunt grimly. 'Let us hope you are getting sense.'

'Or a wise tooth,' says Colonel Neilson, with a friendly smile at Tita. 'Lady Rylton is very *nearly* old enough to be thinking of that now.'

'As for that wretched Mrs. Tyneway,' says Miss Gower, taking no notice of him, 'if her husband did so far take the law into his own hands as to make her black and blue, I, for one, should not blame him.'

'That's funny!' says Mrs. Chichester, giving her a saucy little smile.

'What is funny, may I ask?'

'To hear you defend a man. I thought you despised them in a body.'

'I have my own views about them,' says Miss Gower, with a sniff. 'But I admit they have rights of their own.'

'Fancy allowing a man to have rights

nowadays !' cries Mrs. Chichester, uplifting her long arms as if in amazement. 'Good heavens! What a wife you would have made! Rights ?' She looks up suddenly at Captain Marryatt, who is, as usual, hanging over the back of her chair. 'Do you think a man has any rights ?'

'If you don't, I don't,' returns that warrior, with much abasement and perhaps more sense than one would have expected from him.

'Good boy,' says she, patting his hand with her fan.

'I suppose husbands have some rights, at all events ?' says Sir Maurice.

He says it quite lightly—quite debonnairly, yet he hardly knows why he says it. He had been looking at Tita, and suddenly she had looked back at him. There was something in the cold expression of her face, something defiant, that had driven him to make this foolish speech.

'Husbands ? Pouf! They least of all,' says Mrs. Chichester, who loves to shock

her audience, and now finds Miss Gower
ready to her hand.

'Where is your husband now, Mrs.
Chichester?' asks Colonel Neilson, quite
without *malice prepense.*

Margaret gives him a warning glance,
just a little too late. Though indeed, after
all, what is there to warn about Mrs.
Chichester? She is only one of a thousand
flighty young women one meets every day,
and though Captain Marryatt's infatuation
for her is beyond dispute, still, her infatuation for him has yet to be proved. Margaret
had objected to her, in her own mind, as a
companion for Tita—Tita, who seems too
young to judge for herself in the matter of
friendships.

'I don't know, I'm sure,' returns Mrs.
Chichester, lifting her shoulders. 'Miss
Gower will tell you; she knows everything. Miss Gower,' raising her voice
slightly, and compelling that terrible old
woman to look at her, 'will you tell Colonel
Neilson where my husband is now?'

Poor Colonel Neilson! who is beginning to wish that the earth would open and swallow him up.

'It argues ill for you that you should be obliged to ask such a question,' says Miss Gower, with a lowering eye.

'Does it? How dreadful!' says Mrs. Chichester. She looks immensely amused. 'Do you know I heard the other day that he was married again! It can't be true— can it?'

She appeals once again to Colonel Neilson, as if enjoying his discomfiture, and being willing to add to it through pure mischief. However, she is disappointed this time. Colonel Neilson does not know what to do with her appeal to him, and remains discreetly silent. He can see she is not in earnest.

'At all events, *if* true,' says Mrs. Chichester, looking now at Miss Gower, and speaking in a confidential tone, 'I am sure John will let me know about it.'

'John' is Major Chichester.

Marryatt is leaning now so far over her that he is whispering in her ear.

'Is this—*is* this true?' questions he, in low but vehement tones.

'It—it may be. Who can tell?' returns she, with beautiful hesitation.

She subsides once again behind the invaluable fan. To him she seems to be trembling. To Margaret, who is watching her angrily, she seems to be laughing.

'You have evidently great faith in your husband,' says Miss Gower, with what she fondly believes to be the most artful sarcasm.

'Oh, I have — I have!' says Mrs. Chichester, clasping her hands in an enthusiastic fashion.

'And he in you, doubtless?'

'Oh, *such* faith!' with a considerable increase in the enthusiasm.

Miss Gower looks at her over her spectacles. It is an awful look.

'I shall pray for you to-night!' says she, in a piously vindictive tone.

'Oh, thanks! Thanks! How *kind* of you!' says Mrs. Chichester, with extreme pathos.

There is an explosion on her left. Mrs. Chichester looks mournfully in that direction to see the cause of it. There is only Mr. Gower to be seen! He, as usual, is misconducting himself to quite a remarkable degree. He is now, in fact, laughing so hard but so silently that the tears are running down his cheeks. To laugh out loud with his aunt listening, might mean the loss of seven hundred a year to him.

'What's the matter with you? Aren't you well?' asks Mrs. Chichester, in a loud voice, calculated to draw attention to him.

She feels that here is an opportunity given her to pay off old scores.

'Oh, don't!' gasps Gower, frantically struggling still with his laughter. 'If she hears you, she'll be down on me like a shot. As you are strong, be merciful!'

'Very well; remember you are in my

debt,' says she, who *au fond* is not ill-
natured. At this moment Tita passes
down the balcony to where her husband is
standing on the top of the steps that lead
to the gardens beneath.

As she draws closer to him, he fixes his
eyes upon her as if to compel a glance
from her in return; but Tita, who is ac-
companied by Minnie Hescott, does not
so much as once let her gaze wander in
his direction. She comes nearer — ever
nearer, laughing and talking gaily, and
passes him, still without recognition of any
sort. As her skirt sweeps against him, he
speaks.

'Are you going out, Tita?'

It is the first word that has passed
between them since last night—since she
left his room. A sudden angry determination to *make* her speak to him, induces
him now to get before her, and bar her
passage to the steps.

'Yes,' returns she coldly, graciously,
briefly.

She leans back a little, as if to catch up the tail of her white gown—in reality, to avoid looking at him.

'Just here there is shelter,' says Rylton, speaking hurriedly, as if to gain time, and keep her from gliding past him. 'But outside—— And you have a very thin frock on. Shall I get you a shawl?'

'No, thank you.'

Her manner is still perfectly gracious, but still she refuses to look at him. The gathering up of her frock is evidently causing her a great deal of trouble.

'Shall I take you out some cushions, then?'

'No, thank you.'

She has conquered the frock now, but still she does not look at him. In fact, she turns to Minnie, and, as though forgetful of his presence, murmurs some little thing or other to her.

'If you are going to the gardens,' says . Rylton, with Heaven knows what intention—perhaps a desire to show her how

little he cares for her childish anger, perhaps
to bring matters to their worst—to know
what she means—'may I come with you?'

Tita gives him a glance—the fleetest; a
smile—the briefest.

'*No*, thank you,' says she, a faint
emphasis upon the 'No' being the only
change in her even tone.

As she speaks she goes down the steps,
Minnie Hescott following her.

CHAPTER XXVIII.

HOW MINNIE HESCOTT GIVES TITA A HINT;
AND LEARNS THAT HINTS MAY BE THROWN
AWAY; AND HOW MARGARET'S SOUL IS
GRIEVED.

MINNIE HESCOTT, during the time it takes
her to go down the terrace steps behind
Tita, comes to a resolution. *She will give
Tita a hint!* It will be a gift of no mean
order, and whether it be well received or
not, will always be a gift to be remem-
bered, perhaps with gratitude.

And Minnie, who is strictly practical if
nothing else, sees a fair hope of return in
her present plan. She likes Tita in her
way—likes her perhaps better than she

likes most people, and Tita may be useful
to her as Sir Maurice Rylton's *wife*.   But
Tita, dismantled of her honours, would be
no help at all, and therefore to keep Tita
enthroned is now a very special object with
her astute cousin.

In and between all this is Minnie's
detestation of Mrs. Bethune, who has
occasionally been rude to her in the small
ways that make up the sum of life.

Minnie, who is not sensitive, takes the
bull by the horns.

'Mrs. Bethune,' says she, as they go by
a bed of hollyhocks now hastening to their
death, 'is a friend of yours?'

It is a question.

'Mrs. Bethune!' says Tita, stopping and
looking at her as if wondering.

What does she mean?

'Yes,' says Minnie pleasantly.   'A
friend.   An old friend!'

'Not an *old* friend,' says Tita quietly.
'She is a cousin of Maurice's.'

'Yes.   But not a friend of yours?'

'No,' coldly.

'I'm glad of that,' says Minnie, with hilarity. 'I *hate* old friends, don't you? They always cost one such a lot. They tell one such horrid news about one's self. They do such nasty things. Give me a stranger for choice. And as for Mrs. Bethune, now you have told me she is not a friend of yours, I suppose I may speak freely. Do you know, Tita, I'd keep my eye on her if I were you. You have given me a free hand, so I can tell you what is in my mind. That woman—she means——'

'What?' asks Tita, turning upon her with some haughtiness.

'*Business!*' says Minnie Hescott, with an emphatic nod. 'Mischief all through. She's up to mischief of some sort. I tell you what,' says Minnie, with her old young look, 'you've *got* to keep your eye on her.'

'I could never keep my eye on anyone,' says Tita, with a sudden, irrepressible little laugh. 'And why should I keep my eye on Mrs. Bethune ? To tell you a solemn truth, Minnie, I can't bear to look at her. She's beautiful, so they say, but to me she is hideous. Therefore, why should I keep my eye on her ? It,' with a whimsical little glance, ' would hurt me so.'

' Nevertheless, you *should !*' says Minnie solemnly. ' She's a viper !'

' Vipers are ugly.'

' And dangerous.'

' Then why look at them ?'

' To avoid them—lest they sting you,' says Minnie, feeling quite pleased with herself for this flight of fancy.

' You think,' says Tita, stopping and looking at her, ' that Mrs. Bethune will sting me ?'

' I think nothing,' says Minnie Hescott, throwing out her hands in an airy fashion ; ' only, get rid of her—get rid of her, Tita, as soon as ever you can !'

' To get rid of a guest ! *No,*' says Tita. ' She may stay here, and I shall make her welcome for ever——' She pauses and

looks full at her cousin. There is great
courage and great pride in her look. 'For
ever!' repeats she.

'There is always a fool somewhere!' says
Minnie Hescott, with a sigh. 'Well,'
abandoning the discussion for the present,
'let us go for our walk round the garden.'

As they pass beneath the balcony, Margaret, who is leaning over it, with Colonel
Neilson beside her, makes a little irrepressible movement.

'What is it now?' asks he, who knows
every mood of hers.

'Nothing. I was only thinking about
Tita.'

'A charming subject.'

'Oh! *too* charming,' says Margaret, with
a sigh. 'That child troubles me.'

'But why? She seems to be getting on
all right, in spite of your evil prognostica-
tions before her marriage. She and Rylton
seem on very good terms.'

'Not to-day, at all events,' shaking her
head.

'No? I confess I did think there was a little rift somewhere.'

'Oh yes! There is something,' says Margaret somewhat impatiently. 'Did you see the poor child's eyes, and her whole air? Her pretty little attempt at unconcern?'

'I thought Rylton looked rather put out, too.'

'I didn't look at him. I have no patience with him. It was a mad marriage for any man to make.' She pauses. 'I am afraid there was some disagreeableness last night.' She hesitates again. Though quite determined never to marry Colonel Neilson or any other man, she permits herself the luxury of retaining Neilson as a confidential friend. 'I wish her cousin, Mr. Hescott, was not quite so attentive to her. She is very young, of course, but I don't think she ought to have danced so much with him last night.'

'And what of Rylton?' asks the Colonel, pulling the glass out of his eye and sticking

it in again in an angry fashion. 'Who did
he dance with ?'

'Yes. I saw,' sadly.

'Well, why should he complain, then ?'
says Neilson, who can see the right and
the wrong so *much* better because it is not
his own case. 'To tell you the truth,
Margaret, I think Mrs. Bethune should
not be here.'

'I think that, too. But it appears it
was Tita who invited her.'

'My dear girl, who else ? But there is
such a thing as coercion.'

'It was the prettiest, the most cordial
letter. I read it.'

'Then you think she knows nothing of
that old affair ?'

'Old ?' She looks quickly at Neilson.
Do you think it is old—worn out, I
mean ?'

'No, I don't,' says Neilson promptly.
'And in my opinion, the sooner Mrs.
Bethune terminates her visit the better for
everyone.'

'What an unhappy marriage!' says
Margaret, with a sigh. 'All marriages
are unhappy, I think.'

'Not a bit of it. Most of the married
people we know would not separate even
were the power given them to do so.'

'That is merely because they have grown
necessary to each other.'

'Well, what is love?' says Neilson, who
is always defending his great cause against
Margaret's attacks. 'Was there ever a
lover yet, who did not think the woman
he loved necessary to him?'

'It is not the higher form of love,' says
Margaret, who still dreams of an ideal,
born of her first attachment—an ideal that
never in this practical world could have
been realized, and if it *could*, would have
been condemned at once as tiresome to the
last degree.

'It is high enough for most people,' says
Neilson. 'Don't grow pessimistic, Margaret. There is a great deal of light and
joy and laughter in the world, and I know

no one so framed to enjoy it as yourself, if only you would give yourself full sway. You condemn marriage, yet how can you speak of it with authority—you who have not tried it ?'

' Oh, do, *do* stop,' says Margaret, lifting her hand. 'You are getting on that—that wretched old tack again.'

' So I am. I know it. I shall be on that tack to the end of my life. And I think it so unfair of you to condemn any-body without even a hearing.'

' Why, I must,' says she, laughing in spite of herself.

' No, you needn't. Marry me, and then give judgment !'

' I shall never marry,' says Margaret, with cold decision ; then, as if ashamed of her tone, she looks up at him. It is rather a shy look, and makes her even more admirable in the eyes of the man watching her. ' *Why* will you persist ?' asks she.

' I must. I must.'

' It sounds like a doom,' says she lightly,

though tears are gathering in her eyes.
' Don't waste your life. *Don't !'*

' I am not wasting it. I am spending it
on you,' says the Colonel, who is really a
delightful lover.

' Ah ! but that is so dreadful—for me !'

' Do I worry you, then ?'

' No ! no ! A thousand times no !' cries
she eagerly. ' It is only that I must always
reproach myself.'

' Why always ? Give in, Margaret, and
let me change my place from lover to
husband.'

' It is often a fatal change.'

' You mistrust me ?'

' You ! No, indeed ! You least of all.
I believe in you from my very soul ! Don't
think that, Harry. But,' impatiently, ' why
go over it again and again ?'

Colonel Neilson turns a solemn face to
hers.

' Margaret !' says he. ' Are you bent on
dying an old maid ?'

Miss Knollys flushes ; she turns aside.

'What an odious word !' says she.

She walks deliberately into the drawing-room behind her. Neilson still stands leaning over the balcony—a slow and distinctly satisfied smile crosses his features.

CHAPTER XXIX.

HOW TITA COMMITS A GREAT FOLLY, THOUGH LITTLE IS THE SIN THAT LIES THEREIN. AND HOW MARGARET TRIES TO MAKE PEACE, AND WHAT COMES OF IT.

BREAKFAST is nearly over—an uncomfortable breakfast, with only a host to guide it —the hostess had put in no appearance. This would be nothing if the plea of headache had been urged, but headache had been out of it altogether. In fact, Lady Rylton had gone out riding at eight o'clock with her cousin, Mr. Hescott, and has not yet come back, though the clock points at ten-thirty.

Sir Maurice had made very light of it.

He had asked Mrs. Bethune to pour out
the tea, and had said that Tita would be
back presently.   But everyone can see
that he is upset and angry, and Margaret,
noting it all, feels her heart grow cold
within her.

As a fact, Rylton is feeling something
more than anger.   Something akin to
fear.   Where is she—the girl he had
married, meaning to be true to her if
nothing else?   He had questioned her
maid very casually, very unconcernedly,
and she had told him that her mistress
had gone out riding this morning about
eight o'clock with Mr. Hescott.   His
questions had been so clever, so altogether without anxiety, that the maid had
believed in him, and saw nothing in his
words to dwell upon later.

Yet Rylton's heart had seemed to cease
beating as she answered him.   She had
gone riding with Hescott.   With Hescott!
Will she ever come back?

Tita's face, when she had left him that

last night, is before him now. Tita's determination not to accept the olive branch he offered her yesterday is before him too. What if she——'

And, in truth, Tita *had* been angry. Her spirit had been roused. His open declaration that he believed her capable of carrying on a flirtation with her cousin had hurt her more than she cared to confess even to herself. It was so silly—so unjust! She—*she!*

And he! What of him? Everything that his mother had told her of his affection for Marian grew, all at once, fresh in her mind. How did he then *dare* to speak to *her* of inconstancy? He—who had been false to her from the very beginning. When he had spoken to her to-day, as she passed him on her way to the garden, she had felt as though she could hardly bring herself to answer him —and always revenge was in her mind. Revenge—to show him how little she cared for his censures.

When, therefore, Hescott during the evening asked her to go for a ride with him before breakfast next morning, she had said yes quickly — so quickly, that Hescott foolishly believed she meant more than a readiness to ride in the early morning. Did she wish to be *with* him? A mad hope made his heart warm.

As for Tita—she thought only of that small revenge. She would go for a ride with Tom, without telling Maurice one word about it. She could easily be back in time for breakfast, and no one, therefore, would be annoyed, except Maurice! It seemed *delightful* to annoy Maurice !

    *   *   *   *   *

The little revenge hardly seems so delightful now, however, as she springs from her horse, and running into the hall, followed by Hescott, sees by the clock there that it is just half-past ten.

'Oh! you should have *told* me,' cries she, most unjustly turning upon Tom.

'Good heavens! How could I? I

didn't know myself.   I told you I had left
my watch on my dressing-table.'

'Well, we are in for it now, any way,'
says she, with a little nervous laugh.

She walks straight to the breakfast-
room, and, throwing open the door, goes
in.

'I'm so sorry!' says she at once.

She gives a little general, beaming smile
all round.   Only Margaret can see the
nervousness of it.   She had taken off her
hat in the hall, and her pretty, short hair
is lying loosely on her forehead.   There is
a tiny dab of mud on her cheek, close to
the eye.   It is distinctly becoming, and
looks more like a Queen Anne patch than
anything else.

All the men rise as she enters, except
Rylton, who is reading a letter of such
deep importance, evidently, that he seems
hardly to note his wife's entrance.   Tita
beckons to them all to resume their seats.

'I'm dreadfully sorry—dreadfully,' says
she, in a quick little way.   'I had no idea

it was so late.   So *good* of you,' turning to
Mrs. Bethune, who is sitting at the head
of the table, ' to take my place !   You see,'
looking once again round her, ' when I
started I did not mean to go so far.'

'Ah ! that is what so often happens,'
says Mrs. Bethune, with a queer little
glance from under her lids.

There is something so insolent both in
her meaning and her voice, that Margaret's
face flushes, and she makes a slight movement as if to rise ; but Colonel Neilson,
who is next her, by a slight gesture
restrains her.   She looks at Maurice, however, as if wondering why he does not
interfere—does not *say* something ; but
Maurice seems more than ever buried in
his letter.   Indeed, beyond one brief glance
at his wife, he has taken no notice of
her.

Margaret's eyes go back to Tita.   Everyone is offering her a seat here or there,
and she is shaking her head in refusal.
Evidently Mrs. Bethune's remark has gone

by her, like the wind unheard; it had not been understood.

'Come and sit here, and have a hot cup of coffee,' says Captain Marryatt.

'No, thank you. I couldn't really. See how muddy I am,' glancing down at her skirt. 'It must have rained a great deal last night. Tom and I ran a race, and this is the result. I must go upstairs and change my things.'

'Certainly, a change would be desirable in many ways,' says old Miss Gower, in her most conscious tone, on which her nephew, who is helping himself to cold pie on the sideboard, turns and looks at her as if he would like to rend her.

'Yes, run away, Tita; I'll be up with you in a moment,' says Margaret gently, fondly. 'I am afraid you must feel very damp.'

'I feel very uncomfortable, any way,' says Tita, though without *arrière pensée.* Mrs. Chichester, dropping her handkerchief, gets her laugh over before she picks it up again.

Tita moves towards the door, and then looks back. 'Maurice,' says she, with a courage born of defiance, 'will you send me up some breakfast to my room ?'

Sir Maurice turns at once to the butler.

'See that breakfast is sent up to Lady Rylton,' says he calmly.

A faint colour rises to Tita's forehead. She goes straight to the door. Randal Gower, who is still at the sideboard, hurries to open it for her.

''There's a regular ta-ra-ra waiting for *you*,' says he, 'in the near bimeby.'

Tita gives him an indignant glance as she goes by, which that youth accepts with a beaming smile.

Tita has hardly been in her room twenty minutes, has hardly, indeed, had time to change her clothes, when Margaret knocks at the door.

'May I come in ?' asks she.

'Oh ! come in. Come in !' cries Tita, who has just dismissed her maid. She runs to Margaret and kisses her on both cheeks. 'Good-morning,' says she. And then saucily, 'You have come to read me a lecture?'

'No. No, indeed,' replies Margaret earnestly. She *had* perhaps, but the sight of the child's small, pretty, entreating face has done away with everything con-demnatory that was in her mind. Still, there is such a thing as a word in season. 'But, Tita dearest,' says she, 'is it wise, the way you are going on?'

'Ah! I knew I should not escape,' says Tita whimsically.

'I am not going to scold you, really,' says Margaret, smiling; 'but consider, dear child! To begin with——'

'Oh, this is *worse* than I thought,' interrupts Tita, covering her face with her hands, and blinking at her through her fingers. 'Is it going to be firstly, secondly, thirdly? Come to the thirdly at once.'

'Do you know what you want?' says Margaret, who feels fonder of her every moment. 'A good *slap!* I shall deliver it some day. But, seriously now, Tita, you ought to have considered your guests, at all events. If you had stayed in your room it would have been nothing—but——'

'But because I stayed in the open air it was *something!*' Tita bursts out laughing. 'Oh, isn't it funny?' says she. 'It would have been all right if I had had a bad headache. *Either* way they wouldn't have seen me at breakfast, and what it amounts to is, that they are very angry because I hadn't a bad headache.'

'No one is angry at all.'

'No one?'

'Except Maurice, and surely he has some right on his side. You know your conduct was a little—just a little—er——'

'Rude,' says Tita, helping her out. 'Well, I know that, and I am sorry to my heart's core, Margaret, if I was rude—*to you!*'

The climax is very sweet. Margaret tells herself that Tita is too much for her. The girl by this time has her arms round her neck.

'Don't mind me,' says Margaret, holding the little form closely to her. 'Think
of yourself, my dearest. As if *I* should
misunderstand you ! But you should study
conventionality a little ; you should——'

She breaks off; it almost seems to her
that she is preaching deception to this
baby.

'Now, I'll tell you,' says Tita, leaning
back a little from her, and pointing each
word by a tap on her shoulder, 'I'm not
so bad as I *seem !* I really *meant* to be
in, in time for breakfast—but Tom——'

'Tom,' impatiently, 'is a bad adviser !'

'It wasn't his fault, any way. The fact
is, I took it into my head to run a race
with him. He is always lauding that old
horse of his, you know——'

'I don't know. All I do know is, that
Mr. Hescott must have had a watch about
him.'

'Well,' triumphantly, 'he hadn't. So
you don't know anything after all, you
darling old Madge ! He had forgotten it.

He had left it at home! That was just
what put us out! Not that I *care*. Well,
I was going to tell you about our race.
We started for Clumber's Hill—to get
there and back again, and all went well
until my mare ran away with me!'

'Ran away——'

'Don't look like that. I *love* a horse to
run away with me; and there were no
sandpits or precipices of any sort; it was
a real *good* run away. Oh!' throwing out
her arms, 'how I enjoyed it!' She pauses.
'But I don't think Tom did. He was like
an egg when he came up with me. *So*
white!'

'Never mind Mr. Hescott, go on.'

'Well, that's all. By the time I had the
mare well in hand again, we were a good
many miles farther from here than we
meant to be, and, of course, I was late.'
She puts Margaret away from her a little,
and looks at her. 'After all,' says she,
'why should Maurice be so angry about
it? Everyone makes mistakes now and

then. I suppose,' lightly, 'even the immaculate Maurice can make his ?'

'No doubt,' says Margaret, in a low tone.

Is he not making a mistake now—a dreadful one ?

'And, for the matter of that, so can *you*,' says Tita audaciously, but so lovingly that no one could be angry with her.

'Don't waste time over me,' says Margaret, growing very red, but laughing. 'Come back to your naughty little self. Now what are you going to do about this, Tita ?'

'Do ?'

'Yes. Couldn't you go down and say something pretty to Maurice ?'

'Go down—to Maurice ? Go and beg his pardon. Is *that* what you mean ? No, thank you !'

'But, my dear, he is your husband ?'

'Is that all ?' Tita tilts her chin airily. 'One would think I was his daughter, the way you speak, or his slave ! No. I shan't apologize to him, Margaret, if that is what you mean. I'm *hanged* if I do !'

' Tita — my dear !' Margaret looks shocked. ' I don't think you ought to use such expressions. You make me very unhappy when you do.'

' Do I ?' Tita gives her a little sidelong glance, meant to be contrite, but too full of mischief to be anything but incorrigible. ' Then *I'm hanged* if I say it again,' says she.

' Tita, you will come to grief yet,' says Margaret, laughing in spite of herself. ' Now to return to our argument. I tell you, you owe Maurice something for this escapade of yours, innocent as it is. Fancy in what an awkward position you placed him with your guests ! A man doesn't like to feel awkward ; and he is, naturally, a little annoyed with you about it. And——'

' Nonsense !' says Tita ; ' the guests have nothing to do with it ! As if I didn't know ! Maurice is just in a bad temper because I have been riding with Tom. He hates poor old Tom. If I had gone riding with Randal or any of the others, and hadn't been in till *luncheon*, he would have said nothing—he would have treated it as a joke, I dare say.'

'Well—but, Tita, is there nothing in his objection to Mr. Hescott? You must admit, dearest, that your cousin is a little —well, attentive to you.'

'Why, of course he is attentive to me. He is quite like a brother to me.'

'Brothers, as a rule, are not so very attentive to their sisters. The fact is, Tita,' says Margaret desperately, 'that I think—er—that Maurice thinks—that Mr. Hescott is——'

'In love with me? I know that,' says Tita, without the faintest embarrassment. '*Isn't* it absurd? Fancy Tom being in love with *me!*'

Margaret tells herself that she could fancy it very easily, but refrains from saying so.

'How do you know he isn't?' asks she slowly.

'Why, if he was, I suppose he would tell me so,' says Tita, after which Miss Knollys feels that further argument would be useless.

Suddenly Tita turns to her.

'You think me entirely in the wrong,' says she, 'and Maurice altogether in the right. But there are things about Maurice I do not understand. Is he true or is he false? I never seem to know. I don't ask much of him—not half as much as he asks of me—and still——'

'What do you mean, Tita?' asks Margaret, a nervous feeling contracting her throat.

Has she heard, then?—does she know?

'I mean that he is unfair to me,' says Tita, standing back from Margaret, her eyes lighting. 'For one thing, why did he ask Mrs. Bethune to pour out tea this morning in my absence? Was there,' petulantly, 'no one else to ask?'

' She is his cousin.'

' So are you.'

' My dear, I am not married.'

' More shame for you,' says Tita, with the ghost of a smile. ' Well, there was Miss Gower !'

' She is not married, either.'

' And no shame to anyone.' Here Tita, in spite of her wrath, cannot help laughing. ' But really, Margaret, the blame should not be entirely on my side. If I have to accuse Maurice——'

' Accuse him ! Of what ?'

Tita looks full at her.

' You are a good friend,' says she ; ' but his mother told me.'

CHAPTER XXX.

TITA, going down the stairs after her interview with Margaret, meets Randal in the
hall below.

'You look rather down on your luck !'
says he.

'My looks belie me, then,' says she
stoutly. 'But you—what is the matter
with you ?'

'Ruin !' says Mr. Gower tragically.
'My looks do *not* belie me.'

'Good gracious, Randal !'

'Ruin stares me in the face,' says he,
'look where I will.'

'Very rude of it,' says Tita, with an irrepressible laugh. 'One should never stare people out of countenance. You should speak to Ruin.'

'Oh, it's all very fine making a joke of it!' says Mr. Gower, who is, however, laughing too.

'Where are you going now?' asks Tita, as he moves away from her towards the hall door.

'"Anywhere — anywhere out of the world,"' quotes he, with a dismal shake of the head.

'Is it so serious as all that?' cries Tita. 'Look here, Randal; wait a moment, can't you? I have a last request to make. If you *are* bent on dying, do it; but do it nicely—be picturesque: something original, and no blood. Promise me there will be no blood!'

'"So young, and so untender!"' says Gower, gazing at her with deep reproach.

He seems full of quotations.

'But where are you going, really?'

' Out.'

He pauses.

' Not out of your mind, I hope ?'

' Don't be too sure.'

' Well, wait, and I'll go with you,' says
she, glancing at the stand in the hall where
her garden hat is generally to be found.

' Not to-day,' says Gower ; 'you mustn't
come with me to-day.   I'm going out on
business.'

' Business !'

Mr. Gower and business seem so very
far apart.

'Gruesome business,' repeats he, dropping
his voice to a whisper.   ' I'm going with
my aunt — " my dear, unmarried aunt."
It's my last chance.   I shall do or die to-
day, or else '—an afterthought striking him
—' *she* will.'

' Where are you going with her ?'

' I am taking her,' says Mr. Gower,
looking darkly round him, 'for a row on
the lake. She says she dotes on lakes.
I don't think she will dote on your lake

when she returns, if'—with a murderous eye—' she ever does.'

'Are you going to drown her?' asks Tita, catching him by the arm.

She is laughing still.

'I hope not—I *hope* not,' says Gower gloomily. 'Circumstances *may* be favourable. We must pray for the best.'

He tears himself away from her with a profound sigh, and she is still standing laughing in the hall, when the library door opens, and Rylton comes into the hall.

Her laughter dies quickly. Rylton, after a swift, careless glance at her, goes towards the letter-rack and places a letter in it, then goes back to the library. As he reaches the door, however, he hears little running feet behind him.

'Don't go—don't,' says Tita. She has laid one hand upon his arm, and is looking up at him. 'You are angry with me, and——'

'Angry? No!'

'You are—you know you are! And you want to scold me, and——'

'You are quite mistaken,' says Rylton, shaking off her hand gently, but with decision. 'I have no desire whatever to scold you. Why should I?'

He goes past her into the library, but she follows him—a lovely little penitent— with lowered eyes.

'Do scold me!' says she. 'I was wrong; and I did it on purpose, too.'

'On purpose?'

'Yes,' hanging her pretty head; 'I did it to annoy you! You were so—so nasty about Tom the other night—do you remember? So I wanted to make you *really mad* this time—just for revenge, you know; but, honestly, I didn't mean to be late for breakfast.'

'Didn't you?' drearily.

'No, I didn't; you *must* believe that.' She goes nearer to him, and slips her hand through his arm. 'Maurice!' whispers she. He makes her no answer. She moves

even closer to him, and, leaning her little
head against his shoulder, looks up at him.
'*Do* scold me!' says she again. The tender,
childish voice touches him ; it goes home
to his heart—the heart that is so full of
another. He looks down at her, and,
stooping, lays his lips on hers. It can
hardly be called a kiss ; yet it satisfies *her*,
to whom, as yet, kissing means so little.
'Now I am forgiven,' cries she triumphantly.
' Is *that* your scolding ?'

' I told you I couldn't scold you,' says he.
As he says this he sighs heavily.

'What a sigh !' She pushes him from
her with both hands. 'After all, I believe
you hate me !'

' No, I don't,' says Rylton.

He smiles. After all, why not be friends
with her ? Had he explained that indif-
ference was the word she should have
used for hate, would she be any the wiser ?

' No ?—really ?' She has flung herself
into a chair, and is looking at him with
her hands clasped behind her head. ' Well,'

thoughtfully, 'I don't hate you, either. That's a blessing, isn't it?'

'A great one.'

He feels a little piqued, however, at the nonchalance of her manner. Why should it occur to her that she might hate him? She has, unknowingly certainly, but unquestionably, blocked his way to the fulfilment of his desires, but he—— He changes colour; is he standing in *her* way, then?

'What was that letter you were reading this morning when I came in?'

'A letter?'

He brings himself back to the present with an effort.

'Yes. It was so interesting,' says she, making him a little malicious grimace, 'that you could not spare a moment from the reading of it to acknowledge my presence.'

'It was from my mother.'

'No wonder it was so engrossing,' says Tita naughtily. 'Well——'

'It isn't well; it is ill,' returns he, laughing. 'She says she is coming to stay with us for a week or so on her way to Lady Sarah's.'

'Why is she coming?'

'For our sins, I suppose. I really don't know any other reason.' He casts an anxious glance at her. 'I am afraid that you won't care about it.'

'Well, I shan't,' says Tita frankly; 'but if she wants to come, there is nothing more to be said. What *I* am afraid of is that Marian won't like it.'

'Marian?'

'Yes, Marian. It struck me that she was not very fond of your mother. Was I right?'

'I could not possibly answer for Marian.'

'No?'

'Certainly not.'

'Yet I thought,' with a swift glance, 'that you were the one person in the world who could have told me all about her.'

'You were wrong, then. I have known Marian, and—liked her ; but I think no human being can answer for another's likes and dislikes.'

'Perhaps so.' She looks down thoughtfully. 'When is your mother coming ?'

'To-morrow. I shall run up to town and meet her, and bring her on.'

'You will be back to-morrow night ?'

'Well, she seems to think so ; but I expect she will be tired, and stay in town until next morning. In the meantime,' smiling at her, 'I leave the house and the guests and everything in your charge.'

'How delightful !' cries Tita, clapping her hands.

Rylton turns away.

CHAPTER XXXI.

'SUCH a day to go out on the lake !' says
Mrs. Bethune, with a contemptuous curve
of her lip. ' Really, that old woman must
be as mad as she is disagreeable.'

' Well, she could hardly be *more* so,'
says Mrs. Chichester.

They are all in the oriel chamber, the
windows of which look upon the lake, and
now they can see Randal and Miss Gower
rowing apparently in the utmost peace
across it.

'She has a perfect passion for boating,' says Margaret.

'So I should say. I dare say it seems to her pretty and idyllic.'

'Her passions ought to be at a low ebb by this time,' says Mrs. Bethune with a sneer. She has suffered many things at the old maid's hands.

'Well, let us pray Randal will bring her home in safety,' says Tita, laughing.

'My *dear* Lady Rylton!'

'Heavens—what a prayer!' exclaims Mrs. Chichester.

'Let us say it backwards,' says Captain Marryatt, which is considered such a wonderful departure for him, such a stroke of wit on his part, that everyone laughs in the most encouraging fashion.

'You'll be a reigning wit yet, if you don't look out,' says Mrs. Chichester.

'As you are a reigning toast,' responds he, quite fired by the late ovation.

'Oh, goodness!' says Mrs. Chichester, shrugging up her thin shoulders and cast-

ing a queer glance round her from under
her brows; 'let us take him away quickly,
before he cuts himself with his own smart-
ness.'

'Yes. Come down to the library, it's
warmer there,' says Tita. She leads the
way to the door, and when at it looks back
over her shoulder at her husband. 'Are
you coming, Maurice?'

'In a moment or two. I have a few
letters to write first.'

'And you?' says Tita, looking at Mrs.
Bethune.

'I, too, have some letters to write,'
returns Marian.

Her tone is quite ordinary, but to the
young girl gazing at her there seems something defiant in her eyes and her smile,
What is it in the smile—a sort of hateful
amusement.

Tita leaves the room. She goes out
and down the spiral stairs quite collectedly,
to all appearance, yet she is not aware for
a moment that Margaret's hand is on her

arm.   For the first time—the first time in
all her young and most innocent life—a
sin has touched her soul.   She has learned
to hate—she as yet does not know why—
but she knows she hates Marian Bethune.

As the door closes behind her and her
guests, Rylton turns on Marian.

'Why did you say that?   Why didn't
you go?' says he.

His face is as white as death.   He cannot account to himself for the agitation
that is consuming him.

'Why should I not say what is the
truth?' returns she, her beautiful daring
eyes full on his.   'Why should I go?
Does Lady Rylton demand that all her
guests should be at her beck and call,
morning, noon, and night?'

'She demands nothing,' says Rylton.

The terrible truth of what he is saying
goes home to him.   What has she ever
demanded, that poor child, who has given
him her fortune, her life?   Her little,
sweet, half-pathetic face as she looked

back at him from the doorway is before
him. Her face is often before him now.

'She must be a fool, then,' says Marian
insolently. She takes a step nearer to
him. 'Don't let us talk of her. What is
she to us?' cries she, in a low fierce tone
that speaks of words held back for many
days, words that have been scorching her,
and must find sound at last. 'Maurice!
Maurice! how long is this to go on!'
She takes a step nearer to him, and then,
as if it is impossible to her to hold back
any longer, she flings herself suddenly into
his arms. 'Maurice, speak to me. My
love! My life!' Her words are low,
dispirited, broken by little sobs.

Rylton presses her to him. It is an
involuntary movement, the action of one
who would succour another when in trouble.
His face has lost all colour. He is indeed
as white as death. He holds her. His
arms are round her—round this woman he
has loved so long; it is—it must be a
supreme moment—and yet——

He lays his hands upon her arms, and putting her gently back from him gazes into her drenched eyes. Those eyes so dear, so lustrous. How often has he looked into them, when,

'Soft eyes looked love to eyes which spake again'!

'Marian,' says he. His tone is tenderness itself, yet there is now a sudden strength in it that astonishes him. *She* had had all the strength in those old days. She had dominated him, subduing him by her beauty, her charm. The charm is there still—he knows that as he gazes into her deep eyes, but is it quite as potent? A year ago would she have been standing before him, looking at him as she is looking now with this ineffable passion in her gaze whilst *he* stood too? No. He would have been at her feet, her slave, her lover, to do with as she would. 'Marian, is this wise?'

'Ah! one moment!' entreats she sadly. 'It is so seldom I can see you alone, and

this blessed chance—will you refuse it?
You saw how I dared everything. How
I even risked her suspicion. It was
because I felt I *should* see—*should* speak
with you again.'

'You should consider yourself,' says he
in a dull tone.

He hardly understands himself. Where
is the old, wild longing to be with her,
when others are away, to hold her in his
arms? To kiss her lips—dear willing
lips?

'What do I care about myself?' returns
she vehemently. Her passion has so carried her with it, that she has failed to see
the new wonder in his air, the chill, the
lack of warmth, the secret questioning.
'Ah, Maurice, forgive me! It is so like
you to think of me before yourself. And
I know one *must* think. But will it be
always so? Is there no chance, no hope
—of freedom for you and me? You are
rich now, and if—if——'

'Don't,' says he, in a choked tone.

He almost pushes her from him, but she clings to him.

'I know—I know,' says she. 'It is a dishonourable thought, but thoughts will come. And you——' She catches him by both arms, and swaying her lithe body a little, compels his gaze to meet hers. 'They come to you, too,' cries she in a low tone, soft as velvet, but quick with fervour. 'You, too, long for freedom. Do I not know you, Maurice? Do I not believe in you? You are mine—mine! Oh how I honour you, for your honour to *her!* I think you are the one good man I ever met. If I loved you before your marriage, I love you a thousand times better since. You are mine, and I am yours. And we must wait—wait—but not for long. That girl——'

He releases himself from her by a quick, almost infuriated gesture. At the very instant of his doing so the sound of footsteps coming along the corridor without can be heard. Mrs. Bethune steps quickly to a side-door, and passes noiselessly into a passage that leads her to a back staircase. As she runs along it softly, noiselessly, a great swell of delight lifts her bosom.

He loves her. He loves her still. He had not repulsed her when she had flung herself into his embrace, and this last moment when he had flung her out of it, *that* spoke more than all. He had heard those coming footsteps. He had thought of her—her reputation. That was dear to him. She gains her own room by a circuitous round, breathless, unseen, secure in her belief of her power over him. The insatiable vanity of the woman had prevented her from reading between the lines.

Rylton, detesting himself for the necessity for deception, has just seated himself at a writing-table, when Minnie Hescott enters the room. That astute young woman refrains from a glance round the room.

'Still writing?' says she.

She had told herself when she escaped
from the others that she would do a good
turn to Tita.   She decided upon not caring
what Rylton would think of her.   Men
were more easily appeased than women.
She would square him later on, even if her
plain speaking offended him now; and, at
all events, Tita would be on her side—
would acknowledge she had meant kindly
towards her, and even if all failed still
something would be gained.   She would
have ' been even ' with Mrs. Bethune.

Miss Hescott's vocabulary is filled with
choice sayings, expressive if scarcely
elegant.   Beyond her dislike to Mrs.
Bethune, personally—she might have conquered that—Minnie is very clever—there
is always the fact that Mrs. Bethune is
poor, and poor people, as Minnie has
learned through a hard philosophy, are
never of any use at all.   Mrs. Bethune,
therefore, could never advance her one
inch on the road to social success; whereas
Tita, though she is a mere nobody in her-

self, and not of half as good birth as
Mrs. Bethune, can be of the utmost use
as a propeller.

Tita, by happy circumstances, is the
wife of a real live Baronet, and Tita is
her cousin. Tita has money, and is very
likely to go to town every year in the
season, and what more likely than that
Tita should take her (Minnie) under her
wing next season, present her and marry
her ? Delightful prospect. Her step is
quite buoyant as she approaches Rylton
and says :

' Still writing ?'

' Yes,' returns Rylton leisurely, to whom
Minnie is not dear.

' I'm sorry. I wanted to say something
to you,' says Minnie, who has decided on
adopting the unadorned style of conversation, that belongs as a rule to the young
—the unsophisticated.

' If I can be of the slightest use to
you,' says Rylton, wheeling round on his
chair, ' I shall be delighted.' He had

knocked off the blotting paper as he
turned, and now stoops to pick it up, a
moment that Minnie takes to see that he
has no letter half begun before him, and
no letter finished either, as the rack on the
side of the wall testifies. Minnie would
have done well as a female detective!

'Oh no—no. On the contrary, I wanted
to be of use to you.'

'To me?'

'Yes. You mustn't be angry with me,'
says Minnie, still with the air of the *ingénue*
full about her; 'but I felt ever since the
night before last that I *should* speak to
you.'

'The night before last!'

Rylton's astonishment is so immense
that he can do nothing but repeat her
words. And now it must be told that
Minnie, who had seen that vindictive look
on Mrs. Bethune's face as she went down
the terrace steps on the night of Lady
Warbeck's dance, and had augured ill from
it for Tita and her brother, had cross-

examined Tom very cleverly, and had
elicited from him the fact that he had heard
footsteps behind the arbour where he and
somebody—he refused to give the name—
had sat that night, and that he—Tom—
had glanced round, and had seen and
known, but that he had said nothing of
it to his companion. A mutual hatred for
Mrs. Bethune, born in the breast of Tom
as well as in his sister, had alone compelled
Tom to declare even this much. Minnie
had probed and probed about his companion, as to who she was, but Tom would
not speak. Yet he might as well have
spoken. Minnie knew!

'Yes, that night at Lady Warbeck's. I
know you will think me horrid to say what
I am going to say, and really there is
nothing—only—I am so fond of Tita.'

'It is not horrid of you to say that,' says
Rylton, smiling.

'No. I know that. But that isn't all.
I—am afraid Tita has an enemy in this
house.'

' Impossible,' says Rylton.

He rises, smiling always, but as if to put a termination to the interview.

' No, but listen,' says Minnie, who, now she has entered upon her plan, would be difficult to beat. ' Do you remember when you and Mrs. Bethune were standing on the balcony at Warbeck Towers — that night ?'

Rylton starts, but in a second collects himself.

' Yes,' returns he calmly.

He feels it would be madness to deny it.

' Very well,' says Minnie, ' I was there too, and I went down the steps—to the garden. Your wife went down before me.'

Rylton grows suddenly interested. He had seen Minnie go down those steps—but the other !

' Then ?' asks he ; his tone is breathless.

' Oh, yes—just then,' says Minnie, ' and that is what I wanted to talk to you about.

You and Mrs. Bethune were on the balcony above, and Tita passed just beneath, and I saw Mrs. Bethune lean over for a *second* as it were—it seemed to me a most evil second, and she saw Tita—and her eyes!' Minnie pauses. 'Her eyes were awful! I felt frightened for Tita.'

'You mean to tell me that Mrs. Bethune *saw* Tita that night passing beneath the balcony.'

The memory of his bet with Marian, that strange bet, so strangely begun, comes back to him—and other things too! He loses himself a little. Once again he is back on that balcony; the lights are low, the stars are over his head. Marian is whispering to him, and all at once she grows silent. He remembers it; she takes a step forward. He remembers that too —a step as though she would have checked something, and then thought better of it.

Is this girl speaking the truth? *Had* Marian seen and then made her bet, and then deliberately drawn him step by step to that accursed arbour? And all so quietly—so secretly—without a thought of pity, of remorse !

No, it is not true ! This girl is false—— And yet — that quick step Marian had taken ; it had somehow, in some queer way, planted itself upon his memory.

Had she seen Tita go by with Hescott ? She had called it a fair bet ! Was it fair ? Was there any truth anywhere ? If she had seen them—if she had deliberately led him to spy upon them——

A very rage of anger swells up within his heart, and with it a first doubt—a first suspicion of the honour of her on whom he had set his soul ! Perhaps the ground was ready for the sowing.

'Saw her ? Yes, indeed,' says Minnie, still with the air of childish candour. ' It was *because* I saw her that I was so frightened about Tita. Do you know, Sir Maurice '—most ingenuously this—' I don't think Mrs. Bethune likes Tita.'

'Why should you suppose such a thing ?' says Rylton. His face is dark and lowering. 'Tita seems to me to be a person impossible to dislike.'

'Ah, that is what I think,' says Minnie. 'And it made me the more surprised that Mrs. Bethune should look at her so unkindly. Well,' smiling very naturally and pleasantly, 'I suppose there is nothing in it. It was only my love for Tita that made me come and tell you what was troubling me.'

'Why not tell Tita ?'

'Ah, Tita is a little angel,' says Miss Hescott. 'I might as well speak to the winds as to her. I tried to tell her, you know, and——'

'And——'

He looked up eagerly.

'And she wouldn't listen. I tell you she is an angel,' says Minnie, laughing. She stops. 'I suppose it is all nonsense —all my own folly ; but I am so fond of Tita, that I felt terrified when I saw Mrs.

Bethune look so unkindly at her on the balcony.'

'You are sure you were not dreaming,' says Rylton, making an effort, and growing careless once again in his manner.

Minnie Hescott smiles too.

'I never dream,' says she.

CHAPTER XXXII.

HOW MISS GOWER GOES FOR A PLEASANT ROW
UPON THE LAKE WITH HER NEPHEW; AND
HOW SHE ADMIRES THE SKY AND WATER;
AND HOW PRESENTLY FEAR FALLS ON HER;
AND HOW DEATH THREATENS HER; AND
HOW BY A MERE SCRATCH OF A PEN SHE
REGAINS SHORE AND LIFE.

'How delicious the water looks to-day!'
says Miss Gower, gazing at the still lake
beneath her with a sentimental eye. The
eye is under one of the biggest sun-hats in
Christendom. 'And the sky,' continues
Miss Gower, now casting the eye aloft,
'is admirably arranged too. What a day
for a row, and so late in the season,
too!'

' " Late, late, so late !" ' quotes her nephew, in a gloomy tone.

' Nonsense !' sharply; ' it is not so very late, after all. And even if it were there would be no necessity for being so lugubrious over it. And permit me to add, Randal, that when you take a lady out for a row, it is in the very worst possible taste to be in low spirits.'

' I can't help it,' says Mr. Gower, with a groan.

' What's the matter with you ?' demands his aunt.

' Ah, no matter—no matter !'

' In debt, as usual, I suppose ?' grimly.

' Deeply !' with increasing gloom.

' And you expect me to help you, I suppose ?'

' No. I expect nothing. I hope only for one thing,' says Mr. Gower, fixing a haggard gaze upon her face.

' If it's a cheque from me,' says his aunt sternly, ' you will hope a long time.'

' I don't think so,' sadly.

'What do you mean, sir? Do you think I am a weathercock, to change with every wind? You have had your last cheque from me, Randal. Be sure of that. I shall no longer pander to your wicked ways, your terrible extravagances.'

'I didn't mean that. I wished only to convey to you the thought that soon there would be no room for hope left to me.'

'Well, there isn't *now!*' says Miss Gower cheerfully, 'if you are alluding to me. Row on, Randal; there isn't anything like as good a view from this spot as there is from the lower end!'

'I like the middle of the lake,' says Mr. Gower, in a sepulchral tone. As he speaks he draws in both oars, and leaning his arms upon them, looks straight across into her face. It is now neck or nothing, he tells himself, and decides at once it shall be neck. 'Aunt,' says he, in a low, soft, sad tone—a tone that reduces itself into a freezing whisper, '*Are you prepared to die?*'

' What !' says Miss Gower. She drops the ropes she has been holding and glares at him. ' Collect yourself, boy !'

' I entreat you not to waste time over trivialities ! I entreat you to answer me, and quickly.'

Mr. Gower's voice is now apparently coming from his boots.

' Good gracious, Randal, what do you mean ?' cries the spinster, turning very yellow. ' Prepared to *die !* Why ask me such a question ?'

' Because, dear aunt, your time has come !'

' Randal !' says Miss Gower, trying to rise, ' pull me ashore. Do you hear me, sir ? Pull me ashore at once. Cease your levity.'

' Sit down,' says her nephew sadly. ' Pray sit down. It comes easier sitting than any other way, I have been told.'

' What comes ?' Miss Gower casts a wild glance round her. They are far from the shore, and, indeed, even if they had been nearer to it, no help could reach her, as there is not a soul to be seen, and from where they now are not a glimpse of the house is to be had. ' Randal, would you murder me ?' cries she.

' Oh, dear aunt, what a question !' says Mr. Gower with deep reproach. ' No, far from that. Learn that I, too, am resolved to die !'

' Oh, heavens !' cries Miss Gower, clinging to the sides of the boat. 'What brought me out to-day? And to think insanity should break out, in our family here, for the first time! Unhappy youth, bethink yourself! Would you have my death upon your soul ?'

Here all at once it occurs to her that she has read somewhere of the power of the human eye. *She* has an eye, and it is human ; she will use it! She leans forward and half closes her lids (presumably to concentrate the rays within), and casts upon Gower a glance that she herself would have designated ' fell.' The effect is, perhaps, a little destroyed by the fact

that her big hat has fallen over her left ear,
and that she has put on a diabolic grin—
meant to be impressive—that gives all the
gold with which the dentist has supplied
her, to public view.   Quite a little fortune
in itself !   She speaks.

'How *dare* you !' says she, in a voice
meant to be thunder, but which trembles
like a jelly.   'Take me back at once to
the house !   What *madness* is this !'

She is frightened when she utters the
word ' madness.'   But the present madman
does not seem to care about it.

'Not madness, aunt,' says he, still with
unutterable sadness in look and tone, ' but
sober, terrible *truth !*   Life has ceased to
have charms for me.   I have therefore
resolved to put an end to it !'

'But what of me, Randal !' cries the
spinster in an agonized tone.

'I cannot bear to die alone, dear aunt.
To leave you to mourn my memory !   Such
misery I am resolved to spare you.   We
—*die together !'*

'Randal—Randal, I say, you are out of your mind.'

She has forgotten the power of the eye —everything.

'You are right, dear aunt, I *am* out of my mind,' says Mr. Gower, with the utmost gentleness. 'I am out of my mind with misery! I have, therefore, bored a hole in the bottom of this boat, through which I'—sweetly—'am glad to see the water is swiftly coming.'

He points gently to where he has removed the plug, and where the water is certainly coming into the boat.

'It is rising, I think,' says he softly and very pleasantly.

Miss Gower gives a wild scream.

'Help! help!' yells she. She waves her hands and arms towards the shore, but there is no one there to succour her. 'Oh, Randal, the water is coming in— it's wetting my boots. It's getting on to my petticoats! Oh, my goodness! What shall I do?'

Here she picks up most of her garments ; nay, all of them, indeed, and steps
on to a loose bit of wood lying in the
boat.

'Don't look! don't look!' screams she.
There is a flicker of something scarlet—a
second flicker of something that might be
described as white tuckers of white em-
broidery.

'Look!' says Mr. Gower reproachfully.
'What do you take me for? I'd die first.
Ah!'—turning modestly aside—'how I
have always been maligned!' He sighs.
'I'm going to die now,' says he. 'Go on,
aunt,' in a melancholy tone. 'There is
little time to lose. Perfect your arrangements. The water is rising. I admire
you. I do, indeed. There is a certain
dignity in dying nicely, and without a
sound.'

'I *won't* die!' cries Miss Gower wildly.
'I *won't* be dignified. Ho! there! Help!
help!'

She is appealing to the shores on either

side, but no help is forthcoming. She
turns at last a pale glance on Randal.

'Randal!' cries she, 'you say *you* are
tired of life. But—I—I'm not!'

'This is folly,' says Mr. Gower. 'It is
born of an hour, filled with a sudden fear.
In a few moments you will be yourself
again, and will know that you are glad of
a chance of escaping from this hateful
world that you have been for so many
years reviling. Just think! Only yesterday I heard you abusing it, and now in
a very few moments you will sink through
the quiet waters to a rest this world has
never known.'

'You are wrong. It is *not* folly,' says
Miss Gower wildly. 'I don't want to die.
You do, you say. Die, then! But why
sacrifice me? Oh, goodness gracious,
Randal, the boat is sinking! I *feel* it. I
know it is going down.'

'So do I,' says Gower, with an unearthly smile. 'Pray, aunt, pray!'

'I shan't!' cries Miss Gower. 'Oh,

you wretched boy ! Oh, Randal, what's
the matter with the boat ?'

' It's settling,' says Mr. Gower tragically.
' There is time for a last prayer, dear
aunt.'

Miss Gower gives a wild shriek.

' Forgive me, my beloved aunt,' says
Mr. Gower, with deep feeling. He is
standing up now, and is doing something
in the bottom of the boat. ' Honour alone
has driven me to this deed.'

' Honour ! Randal ! Then it isn't madness. Oh, my dear boy, what is it ? Oh,'
shrieking again to the irresponsive shore,
' will no one save us ?'

' You can !' says Mr. Gower. ' At least
you *could*. I fear now it is too late. I
gave you a hint about that before, but
you scorned my quotation. Therefore,
thy death be on thy own head !'

' Oh, it can't be too late yet. You can
swim, my dear good Randal. My *dearest*
boy ! I can help, you say. But how,
Randal, is it—*can* it be that the debt you

spoke of a while ago has driven you to
this ?'

'Ay, even to this!' says Mr. Gower in
a frenzied tone.

'How much is it, dearest ?   Not *very*
much, eh ?   Your poor old aunt, you
know, is far from rich.'. As a fact, she
hardly knows what to do with her money.
'Oh, speak, my dear boy, speak !'

'It is only seven hundred pounds,' says
Mr. Gower in a voice full of depression.
'But rather than ask you to pay it, aunt,
I would——'   He bends downwards.

'Oh, *don't !*' screams Miss Gower.   'For
Heaven's sake don't make any more
holes !'

'Why not ?' says Randal.   'We all can
die but once !'

'But we can live for a long time yet.'

'*I* can't,' says he.   'Honour calls me.
Naught is left me but to die.'

Here he stands up and begins to beat
frantically upon the bottom of the boat, as
if to make a fresh hole.

'Oh, darling boy, don't! Seven hundred pounds, is it? If that can save us, you shall have it, Randal, you shall indeed!'

'Is that the truth?' says Gower. He seats himself suddenly upon the seat opposite to her, and with a countenance not one whit the less draped in gloom, pulls from his pocket a cheque-book, a pen, and a tiny little ink case.

'I hardly know if there is yet time,' says he, 'but if you will sign this, I shall do my best to get back to a life that is apparently dear to you, though not'—mournfully—'to me.'

Miss Gower takes the pen, plunges it into the ink, and writes her name. It is not until to-morrow that she remembers that the cheque was drawn out in every way, except for her signature.

'Ah, we may yet reach the shore alive!' says Mr. Gower, in a depressing tone, putting in the plug.

When they do reach it, he gives his arm to his aunt, and, in the tenderest fashion, helps her along the short pathway that leads to the house.

In the hall quite a large number of people are assembled, and everyone runs toward them.

'Why, we thought you were lost,' says Mrs. Chichester.

'Yes, so we were very nearly,' says Mr. Gower, shaking his head and advancing into the hall with all the languid airs of one who has just undergone a strange experience.

'But how—how?' They all crowd round him now.

'Poor aunt and I were nearly drowned,' says Mr. Gower pathetically. He takes a step forward, and the water drips from his trousers. He looks back at Miss Gower. 'Weren't we?' says he.

'But you are dripping!' cries Tita, 'whilst Miss Gower seems quite dry. Dear Miss Gower,' turning anxiously to that spinster, 'I hope you are not wet.'

'Ah! she was so nice, so *nice*,' says

Randal sweetly, ' that she wouldn't let me
do much for her. But if you will just
look under her petticoats I am afraid you
will——'

' Randal !' cries Miss Gower indignantly.

After this the spinster is hurried upstairs
by many willing hands and is put to bed.
Tita, on her way down from seeing her
made comfortable, meets Randal redressed
and dry and comfortable in the library.

' What does all this mean ?' says she.
' When you spoke this morning of taking
Miss Gower out on the lake I—I did not
suspect you of anything—but now——'

' Well, now, you shall hear the truth,'
says Gower. Whereupon he gives her a
graphic account of the scene on the lake.

' I knew she'd take *that* fence,' says he.
' And I was right ; there wasn't even a jib.'

' I wonder you aren't ashamed of yourself,' says Tita indignantly.

' Don't wonder any more. I *am* ashamed
of myself. I'm so ashamed that I'm going
at once to pay my debts.'

' Oh, I like that !'

' Well, I am.   I shall give my landlady five pounds out of her account.'

' And the account ?'

' I really think it must be about seventy or eighty by this time,' says Mr. Gower thoughtfully.   ' However, it doesn't matter about that.   She'll be awfully pleased to get the five pounds.   One likes five pounds, you know, when one has lost all hope of ever getting it.'

' Oh, go away !' says Tita.   ' You are a *horrid* boy !'

CHAPTER XXXIII.

HOW ALL THE HOUSE PARTY AT OAKDEAN
GROW FRIVOLOUS IN THE ABSENCE OF THE
LORD AND MASTER; AND HOW MRS. BETHUNE
ENCOURAGES A GAME OF HIDE-AND-SEEK ;
AND HOW, AFTER MANY ESCAPES, TITA IS
CAUGHT AT LAST.

'SHE has gone to bed,' says Tita, re-
appearing in the drawing-room just as
the clock strikes nine on the following
evening.

' Thank goodness !' says Mrs. Chichester,
sotto voce, at which Captain Marryatt
laughs.

' She is not very ill, I hope ?' says
Margaret.

'Oh no!   A mere headache.'

'Bile!' suggests Mr. Gower prettily.

Tita looks angrily at him.

'What a hideous word that is!' says Mrs. Bethune, with a sneer.   'It ought to be expunged from every decent dictionary. Fortunately,' with a rather insolent glance at Randal, who is so openly a friend of Tita's, 'very few people use it—in civilized society.'

'And I'm one of them,' says that young man, with deep self-gratulation.   'I like to be in a minority—so choice, you know; so distinguished!   But what, really,' turning to Tita, 'is the matter with poor, dear old auntie?'

'A chill, I should think,' returns Tita severely.   Has he forgotten all about yesterday's escapade?   'She seemed to me very wet when she got home last evening.'

'She was soaking,' says Mr. Gower. 'She didn't show it much, because when the water was rising in that wretched old boat—really, you know, Maurice ought to put respectable boats on his lake—she pulled up her——'

' Randal !'

' Well, she did !' says Randal, unabashed. ' Don't glare at *me* ! I didn't pull up anything ! I'd nothing to pull up, but she——' Here Mr. Gower gives way to wild mirth. ' Oh, if you'd *seen* her !' says he—' such spindleshanks !'

At this Marryatt gets behind him, draws a silken chair-back over his face, thus mercifully putting an end to his spoken recollections.

' If I were you, Tita, I should order Randal off to bed,' says Margaret, who, I regret to say, is laughing. ' He has been up quite long enough for a child of his years.'

' Well—but, really, what is the matter with Miss Gower ?' asks somebody.

' Temper,' puts in Mrs. Bethune, with a shrug.

She is leaning back in an easy-chair,

feeling and looking distinctly vexed.
Maurice is away. This morning he had
started for town to meet his mother, and
bring her back with him for a short stay
at Oakdean. He had gone away directly
after breakfast, telling them all he would
be home by the evening if possible; but
he feared the journey would be too long
for his mother, and that probably she
would spend the night in town. In the
meantime, if anything in the shape of a
murder or an elopement should occur,
they might telegraph to Claridge's. He
had then turned and smiled at Tita.

'I leave them all in your care,' he had
said.

Was there meaning in his smile—was it
a little entreaty to her to be 'good' during
his absence?

'Well, she's in bed, any way,' says
Tita; 'and the question is, what shall we
do now?'

'Dance!' says someone.

But they have been dancing every

evening, and there seems nothing very special about that.

'I tell you what,' says Tita; 'let us have hide-and-seek!'

'Oh, how lovely!' cries Mrs. Chichester, springing to her feet. 'What a heavenly suggestion!'

'Yes; two to hunt, and all the rest to hide in couples,' says Tom Hescott.

It has occurred to him that he would like to hunt with Tita, or else to hide with her; and it might be managed. Margaret, who happens to be looking at him, makes a slight movement forward.

'Perhaps we should disturb Miss Gower!' says she anxiously.

'Oh no!' says Mrs. Bethune quickly. 'Her room is in the north wing. If we confine our game to this part of the house, she can never hear us.'

'Still, it seems such a silly thing to do!' says Margaret nervously.

She distrusts Marian where Tita is concerned. Why should she advocate this game — she who is the embodiment of languor itself, to whom any sort of running about would mean discomfort ?

' Dear Margaret,' says Mrs. Bethune, in a low voice, but a distinct one—one quite loud enough for Colonel Neilson to hear, who is standing near Miss Knollys— ' don't give way to it ; don't let it conquer you—*too* soon !'

' It ?—what ?' asks Margaret unconsciously.

' Middle age !' sweetly, and softly always, but with a rapid glance at Neilson. She leans back and smiles, enjoying the quiet blush that, in spite of her, rises to Margaret's cheek. ' I feel it coming,' says she. ' Even *I* feel it. But why encourage it ? Why not let these children have their game, without a check from us who are *so* much older ?'

' That is not the question,' says Margaret coldly, who has now recovered herself. ' My thought was that perhaps Maurice might not approve of this most harmless, if perhaps——'

'Frivolous performance. Of course, if
you are going to manage Maurice and
Maurice's wife,' with a strange laugh,
'there is no more to be said. But I wish
you joy of the last task. And as for
Maurice,' with a curl of her lips, '*he* is
not a prig.'

'Well, neither am I, I hope,' says
Margaret, with perfect temper.

She turns away, Colonel Neilson, who
is furious with Mrs. Bethune, following
her. As for the latter, she looks after
Margaret until she is out of sight, and for
once, perhaps, is sorry for her rudeness.
She likes Margaret, but she is out of heart
to-night and irritable. The absence of
Rylton, the coming of her aunt, all tend
to disturb her. And Rylton had gone
without a word, a look even !—he who
always dwelt upon her words, had studied
her looks ; he had not given her one fare-
well sign. She had waited to see if he
would give one to Tita ; but he had not—
at least, nothing in particular—nor had

Tita run out to the hall to see him off. She had blown him a little kiss from behind the urn, which he had accepted calmly, and that was all!

'Come on,' says Randal excitedly; 'Miss Hescott and I will hunt the lot of you! But look here, you must all keep to the parts of the house agreed on. I am not going to have my beloved aunt descending upon me in a nightcap and a wrapper!'

'Well, you must give us three minutes,' says Tita, 'and you mustn't stir until you hear someone cry, "Coo-ee!" You understand now, Minnie.'

'I know! I'll keep him in hand,' says Miss Hescott.

'And he mustn't peep,' says Mrs. Chichester.

'Good gracious! what a mean thought!' says Mr. Gower, who is already laying plans in his own mind as to how he is to discomfit the hiders, and win laurels for himself as a searcher.

'Well, off we go!' cries Mrs. Chichester,

flying out of the room, Captain Marryatt after her.

Hide-and-seek as a game leaves little to be desired. Even Margaret, who had said so much against it, enters into the spirit of it presently, and knows the throes of anguish when the hunter draws nigh her hiding-place, and the glow of joy when she has safely eluded him and flown to the den, without a clutch upon so much as the end of her garments. Indeed, all have given themselves up to the hour and its excitement, except only Marian Bethune, who, whilst entering into the game with apparently all the zest of the others, is ever listening—listening—— He had said he *might* come home to-night. And it is now close on eleven! In ten minutes, if at all, he will be here. If only she could so manage as to——

They are all now standing once more, laughing, talking, in the small drawing-room, preparatory to another start.

'Who'll hunt now?' asks Colonel Neil-

son, who has been far and away the best
pursuer up to this.

'Why not Tita and Mr. Hescott?' says
Marian suddenly, vivaciously. She seems
to have lost all her indolence. 'They
have not been hunting once to-n'ght.'

'Yes; that is true,' says Captain Marryatt.

'I hate hunting and I like hiding,' says
Tita. 'Colonel Neilson, you and Margaret
can be our pursuers this time. Come,
Tom! come, all of you!'

Mrs. Bethune for a moment frowns, and
then a quick light comes back to her eyes.
Even *better* so—if Maurice should arrive.
She had planned that they—those two,
Tita and her cousin—should be together
on his arrival, should he come; and now,
now they will be *hiding* together in all
probability! Oh for Maurice to come
now—now!

She has evaded her own partner in the
game, and, slipping away unobserved, is
standing in one of the windows of the

deserted library—a window that opens on the avenue—listening for the sound of horses' hoofs. In five minutes Maurice will be here, if he comes at all to-night, and as yet they have scarcely started on their game of hide-and-seek. She had heard Tita whisper to Mr. Hescott something about the picture-gallery—she had caught the word—a delightful place in semi-darkness, and with huge screens here and there. Oh, if only Tita could be found hiding behind one with Mr. Hescott!

She presses her hot cheek against the pane of the open window, and as she does so she starts. She leans out into the night, and yes—yes, beyond doubt, here is the carriage!

It is rounding the bushes at the corner, and is already in sight. She springs lightly into the hall—now deserted, as all the house party have gone up the stairs to the happy hunting grounds above. All, that is, except Margaret and Colonel Neilson, who are waiting for the ' Coo-ee.'

Mrs. Bethune had forgotten them, and running lightly through the hall, she opens the door, and steps into the moonlight just as Sir Maurice comes up the steps.

'You!' says he, surprised.

'Yes. I heard you coming.' There is a sort of wild delight in her voice. She would have liked to have flung herself into his arms, but the men outside are busy with his portmanteau and other things; and then—his mother——

'Your mother?' asks she, peering into the darkness.

'She has not come. I had a telegram from her at Claridge's. She can't come till next week, so I came back.' He pauses, and then, abruptly, 'Where is Tita?'

'Tita?' Mrs. Bethune shrugs her shoulders, and a little low laugh escapes her. 'She is playing hide-and-seek,' says she, 'with—her cousin.'

'What are you saying?' exclaims Rylton, her manner far more than her words striking cold to his heart. 'Do you mean to insinuate——'

'Why, nothing. I insinuate nothing ; we have all been playing——'

'All ?'

'Yes.'

'You and——'

'And everyone else.'

'Was there nothing better, then, for you all to do ?'

'Many things,' coldly. 'But your wife started the game. She had doubtless her reasons——'

'Is that another insinuation ? But at all events you cannot condemn the game, as you joined in it.'

'I could not avoid joining in it. Was *I* to be the one to censure my hostess ?'

'Certainly not,' sternly. 'No one is censuring her. And besides, as you all——' Then, as though the words are torn from him, 'Where is she now ?'

'In the picture-gallery, behind one of your favourite screens, with Mr. Hescott.'

'A graphic description,' says he.   He almost thrusts her aside, and steps quickly into the hall.   Mrs. Bethune, leaning against the wall behind her, breaks into silent, terrible laughter.

At the foot of the stairs Margaret comes quickly to him.   His face frightens her.

'Where are you going, Maurice?'

'Upstairs,' returns he quite calmly.

'You are going to be angry with Tita,' says Margaret suddenly.   'I know it! And nothing is true.   *Nothing!*   What has Marian been saying to you?   She '— with the very strangest little burst of passion, from Margaret, the quiet Margaret!—'she has been telling you lies!'

'My dear Margaret!'

'Oh, Maurice, do be led by me!—by *anyone* but her!' says Miss Knollys, holding him, as he would have gone on.   'Why can't you see?   Are you blind?'

'I really think I must be,' returns he with a peculiar smile.   'It is only just now I am beginning to open my eyes.

My dear, good Margaret!' He lifts her
hand from his sleeve and pats it softly.
'You are too good for this world. It is
you who are blind, really. It will take
longer to open your eyes than even mine.'
He runs lightly past her up the stairs.

Margaret gives a little cry of despair.
Colonel Neilson, catching her hand, draws
her into a room on the left. The expected 'Coo-ee' has been called twice
already, but neither Margaret nor Neilson
have heard it.'

'Marian has done this,' says Margaret,
in great distress. He has her hand still
in his, and now, half unconsciously, she
tightens her fingers over his.

'That woman is a perfect devil!' says
the Colonel savagely. 'She is playing
Old Harry with the *régime* here.'

'I can't think what she means to be the
end of it,' says Margaret. 'She can't
marry him herself, and——'

'She might, you know, if—if—she could
manage to prove certain things.'

'Oh *no!* I won't believe she is as bad as that,' says Margaret with horror. 'She has her good points. She has, really, though you will never believe me.'

'Never!' says the Colonel stoutly. 'The way she behaved to you this evening——'

'To me?' Margaret flushes quickly. The flush makes her charming. She knows quite well to what he is alluding, and she likes him for being indignant with Marian because of it—and yet, if only he *hadn't* alluded to it! It isn't nice to be called middle-aged—though when one is only thirty, one ought to be able to laugh at it—but when one is thirty and un-married, somehow one never laughs at it.

'To you. Do you think I should have cared much if she had been beastly to anyone else? I tell you, Margaret, I could hardly restrain myself! I had only one great desire at the moment—that she had been a man.'

'Ah! But if she had been a man, she

wouldn't have said it,' says Margaret.
There is a little moisture in her eyes.

'No, by Jove! of course not. I'll do
my own sex that credit.'

'And after all,' says Margaret, 'why be
so angry with her? There was nothing
but truth in what she said.'

There is something almost pathetic in
the way she says this; she does not know
it, perhaps, but she is plainly longing for
a denial to her own statement.

'I really think you ought to be above
this sort of thing,' says the Colonel, with
such indignation that she is at once com-
forted; all the effusive words of flattery he
could have used could not have been half
so satisfactory as this rather rude speech.

'Well, never mind me,' says she; 'let
us think of my dear little girl. My poor
Tita! I fear—I fear——' She falters,
and breaks down. 'I am powerless. I
can do nothing to help her; you saw how
I failed with him just now. Oh, what
shall I do?'

She covers her face with her hands, and tears fall through her fingers.

Neilson, as if distracted by this sad sight, lays his arm gently round her shoulder, and draws her to him.

'Margaret, my darling girl, don't cry about it, whatever you do,' entreats he frantically. 'Margaret, don't break my heart!'

Miss Knollys' tears cease as suddenly as though an electric battery has been directed at her.

'Nonsense! Don't be foolish! And at *my* age too!' says she indignantly.

She pushes him from her.

CHAPTER XXXIV.

HOW TITA IS 'CAUGHT,' BUT BY ONE WHOM
SHE DID NOT EXPECT; AND HOW SHE
PLAYED WITH FIRE FOR A LITTLE BIT;
AND HOW FINALLY SHE RAN AWAY.

RYLTON, striding upstairs, makes straight
for the picture-gallery. It strikes him as
he passes along the corridor that leads to
it that a most unearthly silence reigns
everywhere, and yet a sort of silence that
with difficulty holds back the sound behind
it. A strange feeling that every dark
corner contains some hidden thing that
could at a second's notice spring out upon
him oppresses him, and, indeed, such a
feeling is not altogether without justifica-

tion.   Many eyes look out at him at these
corners as he goes by, and once the deadly
silence is broken by a titter, evidently
forcibly suppressed!   Rylton takes no
notice, however.   His wrath is still so
warm that he thinks of nothing but the
picture-gallery, and that screen at the end
of it—where *she*, his wife, is——'

Now, there is a screen just inside the
entrance to this gallery, and behind it are
Minnie Hescott and Mr. Gower.   Randal's
eyes are sharp, but Minnie's even sharper.
They both note, not only Maurice's abrupt
entrance, but the expression on his face.

'Do something—quickly,' says Minnie,
giving Randal a little energetic push that
all but overturns the screen.

'Anything!   To half my kingdom; but
what?' demands Mr. Gower, in a whisper
very low, as befits the occasion.

'Tita is down there with Tom,' says
Miss Hescott, pointing to the far end of
the long, dimly-lit gallery.   'Do you want
to see *murder* done?'

'Not much,' says Gower. 'But—how am I to prevent it?'

'Don't you know what you must do?' says she energetically. 'Those idiots downstairs have forsaken us. Run up the room as quick as you can—past Sir Maurice—and pretend you are the one who is hunting. *I'll* go for Tom. If we make a regular bustle, Sir Maurice won't think so much about our little game as he does now. Did you see his face?'

'I saw fireworks,' says Mr. Gower. Then, ' I'm off,' says he.

He slips out from behind the screen, and galloping up the room comes to the screen very nearly as soon as Rylton. Not soon enough, however. Rylton has turned the corner of it, and found Tita with Tom Hescott crouching behind it, whispering together, and evidently enjoying themselves immensely.

As she sees him, Tita gives a little cry. She had plainly taken him for one of the hunters, and had hoped he would pass by.

'Oh, you!' cries she. 'You! Go away. Go *at once !* They'll find us if——'

She waves him frantically from her. He is too angry to see that there is not a vestige of embarrassment in her air.

Here Gower comes up panting.

'Caught!' cries he, making a pounce at Tita.

'Not a bit of it!' says she, springing away from him to the other side of the screen. 'And *you*, Randal, you are not hunting. Where's Colonel Neilson? Where's Margaret?'

'They changed,' says Mr. Gower mendaciously. 'Miss Hescott and I are upon the track ; we are the bloodhounds— we,' making another grab at her soft gown, 'have *got* you!'

'No, you haven't,' says Tita, whereupon there ensues a very animated chase round and round the screen, Tita at last finding shelter—of *all* places—behind her husband —behind Maurice, whose face it is quite as well she cannot see.

He makes a movement as if to go, but she catches him, and unless he were to use violence he could hardly get away.

'There now!' says she, addressing Rylton indignantly. 'See how you've given us away. You've told him where we were. Don't stir. You mustn't. If you do he'll catch me.'

She laughs defiantly at Gower as she says this. Gower could have laughed too. There could, indeed, be hardly anything stranger than the scene as it stands—comedy and tragedy combined. The husband cold, impassive, stern, and over his shoulder the charming face of his little wife peeping—all mirth and fun and gaiety.

'You *must* stay,' says she, giving Sir Maurice a little shake. 'Why, you've betrayed our hiding-place. You've shown him where we were. It isn't fair, Randal —it isn't indeed——'

'You're caught, any way,' says Gower, who would willingly bring the scene to a close.

He can see Maurice's face, she cannot. As for Tom Hescott, his sister has
chased him out of the gallery long
before this, with a promptitude that does
her credit.

'Caught! Not I,' says Tita. 'Caught,
indeed!'

'Certainly you're caught,' says Gower,
making frantic little dabs at her; but she
dances away from him, letting her husband
go, and rushing once more behind the
unfriendly screen that has done her so bad
a turn.

'Certainly I'm *not*,' retorts she, nodding
her saucy head at him. Slowly and art-
fully, as she speaks, she moves towards
the farther end of the screen, always keeping an eye on her adversary over the top
of it until she comes to the far end, when,
darting like a little swallow round the
corner, she flies down the long, dark
gallery. Once only she turns. '*Now* am
I caught?' cries she, laughing defiance at
Gower.

'Call *that* fair, if you like!' says he, in high disgust.

But she is gone.

* * * * *

The house is quiet again. Gower and Marryatt are still lingering in the smoking-room, but for the rest, they have bidden each other ' Good-night ' and gone to their rooms.

Tita is sitting before her glass having her hair brushed, when a somewhat loud knock comes to her door. The maid opens it, and Sir Maurice walks in.

' You can go,' says he to Sarah, who courtesies and withdraws.

' Oh ! it is you,' says Tita, springing up.

Her hair has just been brushed for the night, and round her forehead some cloudy ringlets are lying. She had thrown on her dressing-gown—a charming creation of white cashmere, almost covered with lace —without a thought of fastening it, and her young and lovely neck shows through the opening of the laces whiter than its

surroundings. Her petticoat — all white
lace, too, and caught here and there with
tiny knots of pale pink ribbons—is naturally
shorter than her gown would be, and
shows the dainty little feet beneath them.

> ' When youth and beauty meet together,
>   There's worke for breath.'

And surely here are youth and beauty
met together! Rylton, seeing the sweet
combination, draws a long breath.

She advances towards him in the friend-
liest way, as if delighted.

'I haven't had a word with you,' says
she. 'Hardly one. You just told me
your mother had not come, and'—she
stops, and breaks into a gay little laugh—
'you must forgive me, but what I said to
myself was, "*Thank goodness !*"' She
covers her eyes with widened fingers, and
peeps at him through them. 'What I
said to you out loud was, "Oh, I *am*
sorry!" Do you remember? Now, am I
not a hypocrite?'

At this she takes down her hands from her eyes, and holds them out to him in the prettiest way.

He pushes them savagely from him.

'You are!' says he hoarsely; 'and one of the very worst of your kind!'

CHAPTER XXXV.

HOW TITA, HAVING BEEN REPULSED, GROWS
ANGRY ; AND HOW A VERY PRETTY BATTLE
IS FOUGHT OUT ; AND HOW TITA GAINS A
PRESENT ; AND HOW SIR MAURICE LOSES
HIS TEMPER.

HER hands drop to her sides. She grows
suddenly a little pale. Her eyes widen.

'What is it? What have I done *now* ?'
asks she.

The 'now' has something pathetic
in it.

'Done! done!' He is trying to keep
down the fury that is possessing him. He
had come to speak to her with a fixed
determination in his heart not to lose his

temper, not to let her have that advantage over him. He would be calm, judicial, but now—— What is the matter with him now? Seeing her there, so lovely and so sweet, so full of all graciousness— a very flower of beauty—a little thing—

> 'Light as the foam that flecks the seas,
> Fitful as summer's sunset breeze'—

somehow a very *rage* of anger conquers him, and he feels as if he would like to take her and *compel* her to his will. 'You have done one thing, at all events,' says he. 'You have forfeited my trust in you for ever.'

'*I* have?'

'Yes, you? When I left home this morning, what was the last word I said to you? I must have been a fool indeed when I said it. I told you I left our house and our guests in your charge.'

'Well?'

'Well?' He checks himself forcibly. Even now, when passion is gathering, he holds himself back. 'When I came back what did I see?'

'Our house—*not* in flames, I hope; and our guests—enjoying themselves!' Tita has lifted her head. She allows herself a little smile. Then she turns upon him. 'Ah, I told you!' says she. 'You want always to find fault with me.'

'I want nothing but that my wife should show *some* sort of dignity.'

'I see! You should have asked Mrs. Bethune to see after your house—your guests!' says Tita.'

She says it very lightly. Her small face has a faint smile upon it. She moves to a large lounging chair, and flings herself into it with charming *abandon*, crosses her lovely naked arms behind her head, and looks up at him with naughty defiance.

'Perhaps you hardly know, Tita, what you are saying,' says Rylton slowly.

'Yes, I do. I do indeed. What I do *not* know is, what fault you have to find with me.'

'Then learn it at once.' His tone is stern. 'I object to your playing hide-and-seek with your cousin.'

'With my cousin! One would think,' says Tita, getting up from her chair and staring at him as if astonished, 'that Tom and I had been playing it by *ourselves !*'

'It seemed to me very much like that,' says Rylton, his eyes white and cold.

'I know what you mean,' says Tita. 'And,' with open contempt, 'I'm sorry for you—you think Tom is in love with me! And you therefore refuse to let me have a single word with him at any time. And why ? What does it matter to you, when *you* don't care ? When *you* are not in love with me !' Rylton makes a slight movement. 'It's a regular dog in the manger business ; *you* don't like me, and therefore nobody else must like me. That's what it comes to ! And,' with a little blaze of wrath, 'it is all so absurd, too ! If I can't speak to my own cousin, I can't speak to anyone.'

'I don't object to your speaking to your cousin,' says Rylton; 'you can speak to him as much as ever you like. What I object to is your making yourself particular with him—your spending whole *hours* alone with him.'

'Hours! We weren't five seconds behind that screen.'

'I am not thinking of the screen now; I am thinking of yesterday morning, when you went out riding with him.'

'What! you have not forgotten that yet?' exclaims she, with high scorn. 'Why, I thought you had forgiven, and put all that behind you.'

'I have not forgotten it. I might have considered it wiser to say nothing more about it, had not your conduct of this evening——'

'Nonsense!' She interrupts him with a saucy little shrug of her shoulders. 'And as for *hours*—it wasn't hours, any way.'

'You went out with him at eight o'clock——'

'Who told you that ?'

'Your maid.'

'You asked Sarah ?'

'Certainly I did. I had to do something before I asked my guests to sit down to breakfast without their hostess !'

'Well, I don't care who you asked,' says Tita mutinously.

'You went out at eight, and you came home late for breakfast at half-past ten.'

'I explained all that to you,' says Tita, flinging out her hands. 'Tom and I went for a race, and of course I didn't think it would take so long, and——'

'I don't suppose,' coldly, 'you thought at all.'

'Certainly I never thought I was going to get a scolding on my return !'

'A scolding ! I shouldn't dream of scolding so advanced a person as you,' says Rylton—who is scolding with all his might.

'I wonder what you think you are doing now ?' says Tita. She pauses and looks

at him critically. He returns her gaze.
His cold eyes so full of condemnation, his
compressed lips that speak of anger hardly
kept back, all make a picture that im-
presses itself upon her mind. Not, alas!
in any salutary way. 'Well,' says she at
last, with much deliberation and open,
childish vindictiveness, 'if you only knew
how *ugly* you are when you look like that,
you would never do it again!' She nods
her head. '*There!*' says she.

It is so unexpected, so utterly undignified,
that it takes all the dignity out of Rylton on
the spot. It suddenly occurs to him that it
is no good to be angry with her. What
is she? A mere naughty child—or——

'You do not know who you are like!'
continues she.

Rylton shakes his head; he is afraid to
speak—a sudden wild desire to laugh is
oppressing him.

'You are the image of Uncle George,'
says she, with such wicked spite that a
smile parts his lips.

'Oh! you can laugh if you like,' says she, 'but you *are*, for all that. You're *worse* than him,' her anger growing because of that smile. ' I never——'

' Never what ?'

' I never met such a *cross cat* in my life !' says Lady Rylton, turning her back on him.

' It's well to be unique in one's own line,' says he grimly.

A short laugh breaks from him. How absurd she is ! A regular little spitfire; yet what a pretty one. His heart is full of sadness, yet he cannot keep back that laugh. He hardly knows how he has so much mirth left in him, but the laugh sounds through the room and drives Tita to frenzy.

' Oh, you can laugh !' cries she, turning upon him. 'You can laugh when— when——' She makes a frantic little gesture that flings open the loose gown she wears, and shows once again her charming neck; words seem to fail her.

'Oh! I should like to *shake* you,' says she at last.

'Would you?' says Rylton. His laughter has come to an end. 'And you. What do you think I should like to do with you?'

He looks at her.

'Oh! I know. It is not difficult to answer,' with a contemptuous glance from under the long, soft lashes, beneath which his glance sinks into insignificance. 'You would like to *give me away!*'

There is a pause.

It is on Rylton's tongue to say she has given *herself* away very considerably of late, but he abstains from saying so—with difficulty, however!

'No, I should not,' says Rylton gravely.

'*No?* Is that the truth?' She bites her lips. 'After all,' with angry tearfulness, 'I dare say it is. I believe you would rather keep me here for ever—just to be able to worry the life out of me day by day.'

'You have a high opinion of me!'

Rylton is white now with rage.

'You are wrong there; I have the worst opinion of you; I think you a tyrant—a perfect *Nero!*'

Suddenly she lifts her pretty hands and covers her face with them. She bursts into tears.

'And you *promised* you would never be unkind to me!' sobs she.

'Unkind! Good heavens!' says Rylton distractedly. *Who* is unkind? Is it he or she? Who is in fault?

'At all events you pretended to be fond of me.'

'I never pretend anything,' says Rylton, whose soul seems torn in twain.

'You did,' cries Tita wildly. 'You *did.*' She brushes her tears aside, and looks up at him—her small, delicate face flushed—her eyes on fire! 'You promised you would be kind to me.'

'I promised nothing,' in a dull sort of way. He feels crushed, unable to move.

'It was you who arranged everything; I was to go my way, and you yours.'

'It was liberal, at all events.'

'And useless!' There is a prophetic note in his voice. 'As you would have gone your way, whether or no.'

'And you, yours!'

'I don't know about that. But your way—where does that lead? Now, look here, Tita '—he takes a step towards her —'you are bent on following that way. But mark my words, bad will come of it.'

'Nothing bad will come of *my* way!' says Tita distinctly.

Her eyes are fixed on his. For a full minute they regard each other silently. How much does she know? Rylton's very soul seems harassed with this question. That old story! A shock runs through him as he says those last words to himself. *Is* it old? That story? *Marian!* What is she to him now?

'As for Tom,' says Tita suddenly, 'I tell you distinctly I shall not give him up.'

'Give him up!' The phrase grates upon his ear. 'What do you mean?' demands he, his anger all aflame again.

'That I shall not insult him, or be cold to him, to please you or anybody.'

'Is that your decision? Then I think it will be wise of your cousin to shorten his visit.'

'Do you mean by that that you are going to be uncivil to him?'

'Yes!' shortly, and with decision.

'You will be cold to him? To Tom? To my own cousin? Maurice, Maurice! Think what you are doing!'

She has come close up to him. Her charming face is uplifted to his.

'Think what *you* are doing,' returns he hoarsely. He catches her hands. 'If you will swear to me that he is nothing to you—nothing——'

'He is my cousin,' says Tita, who hardly understands.

'Oh!' He almost flings her from him. 'There—let it be as you will,' says he bitterly. 'It is your cousin—your house.'

Tita grows very pale.

'That is ungenerous,' says she.

'I have all the faults, naturally.' He goes towards the door, and then suddenly comes back and flings something upon the table before her. 'You once told me you were fond of rings,' says he.

The case has flown open, because of his passionate throwing of it, and an exquisite diamond and pearl ring lies displayed. Tita springs to her feet.

'Oh, wait! *Don't* go! Oh, *do* stop!' cries she, in great distress. '*Fancy* your thinking of me when you were in town! And what a lovely, *lovely* ring! Oh! Maurice—I'm sorry. I am indeed!'

She holds out her hands to him. Rylton, still standing on the threshold of the door, looks back at her.

Is it an apology? An admission that she has been wrong in her dealings with her cousin? An open declaration that this night's undignified proceedings are really being repented of ?

He comes slowly back to her.

' If you are sorry——' begins he.

' Oh, I am indeed. And you must let me kiss you for this darling ring. I know you *hate* me to kiss you—but,' she flings her arms round him, ' I really *must* do it now.'

Instinctively his arms close round her. With a thoroughly astonished air, however, she wriggles herself free, and draws back from him.

' You have done your part beautifully,' says she, with a little soft grimace. ' You bore up wonderfully. I'll let you off next time as a consideration.'

' I don't want to be let off,' says Rylton.

' There, that will do,' lifting her hand. ' And I *am* sorry—remember that.'

' If you are,' says he, ' you will promise me—not to——'

He has grown quite serious again. He hardly knows how to put it into words, and therefore hesitates ; but if only she will cease from her encouragement of her cousin———

'Oh no—never. I shall never do it again,' says she earnestly. 'It was so—so —dreadful of me———'

'If you see it now, I wonder you didn't see 'it then,' says Rylton, a little stiffly ; this sudden conversion brings all the past back to him.

'Well, but I didn't see it then—I always talk too fast.'

She hangs her pretty head.

'I don't remember what you *said*,' says Rylton, a little at fault. 'But—if you are honestly determined, Tita, to be—er—a little more circumspect in that direction in future———'

'I am—I am indeed!' cries Tita. 'I'm sure I can't think how I ever said it to you! It was so rude—so horrid———'

'Said ? *What ?*' demands Rylton, with quick suspicion.

'Well, you know I did call you a *cross*

cat !' says his wife, with a little side glance at him, and a tremulous smile, and withal such lovely penitence, that if he had not been led astray by another thought, he would have granted her absolution for all her sins, here and hereafter, on the spot.

As it is, his wrath grows once more hot within him ; so she is *not* sorry after all.

' Pshaw !' says he.

' Oh, and I called you ugly, too !' cries Tita. ' Oh, how *could* I ? But you will forgive me, won't you ?' She runs after him, and lays her hand upon his arm. ' You do forgive me, don't you ?'

' *No !'* says he violently.

He almost flings her from him.

' Hypocrite !' he says to himself, as he fastens the door of his own room.

A baby's face, and the heart of a liar ! She had played with him ; she had fooled him ; she had, at all events, refused to say she regretted her conduct with her cousin.

He goes down to the garden, feeling it

impossible to sleep just now, and, coming back two hours later, finds the ring he had given her lying on his dressing-table. There is no note with it—not even a single line.

CHAPTER XXXVI.

HOW MRS. BETHUNE IS BROUGHT BEFORE THE
BAR ; AND HOW SHE GIVES HER EVIDENCE
AGAINST TITA ; AND HOW MAURICE'S MOTHER
DESIRES AN INTERVIEW WITH MAURICE'S
WIFE.

'AND now for the news,' says the elder
Lady Rylton next morning, leaning back
in her chair ; she objects to the word
' Dowager.'

Contrary to all expectations, she had
arrived to-day at half-past eight, and is
now, at one o'clock, sitting in her room
with Mrs. Bethune before her. She had
seen Tita, of course ; but only for a
moment or so, as she had been in a hurry

to get to her bedroom and her maid, and
have the ravages that travel had laid upon
her old-young face obliterated. She had,
indeed, been furious (secretly) with Tita
for having come out of her room to bid
her welcome—such bad taste, obtruding
one's self upon a person in the early hours
of the morning, when one has only just
left a train. But what *can* one expect from
a plebeian !

'News ?' says Marian, lifting her brows.

'Well,' testily, 'I suppose there is some !
How is this *ménage* going on ? How is it
being managed, eh ? You have a tongue,
my dear—speak ! I suppose you can tell
me something !'

'Something ! Yes.'

'What does that mean ?'

'A great deal,' says Mrs. Bethune.

'Then you can tell me a great deal.
Begin—begin !' says Lady Rylton, waving
her hand in her airiest style. 'I guessed
as much ! I always hated that girl ! Well
—and so—— *Do* go on !'

'I hardly know what you expect me to say,' says Mrs. Bethune coldly, and with a hatred very badly suppressed.

'You know perfectly well,' says her aunt. 'I wish to know how Maurice and his wife are getting on.'

'How can I answer that?' says Marian, turning upon her like one brought to bay.

It is *too* bitter to her, this cross-examination; it savours of a servitude that she must either endure or—starve!

'It is quite simple,' says Lady Rylton. She looks at Marian with a certain delight in her eyes—the delight that tyrants know. She has this creature at her heels, and she will drag her to her death. 'I am waiting,' says she. 'My good girl, why *don't* you answer? What of Maurice and his wife?'

'They are not on good terms, I think,' says Mrs. Bethune sullenly.

'No? And whose fault is that?' Lady Rylton catches the tip of Marian's gown, and draws her to her. When she has made her turn, so that she can study and gloat over the rapid changes of her face, she says, 'Yours ?' in a light, questioning way.

She smiles as she asks her question—a hateful smile. There is something in it almost devilish — a compelling of the woman before her to remember days that *should* be dead, and a secret that should have been hers alone.

'Not mine, certainly,' says Marian, clearing her throat as though it is a little dry, but otherwise defying the scrutiny of the other.

'And yet you say they are not on good terms!' Lady Rylton pauses as if thinking, and then goes on. 'No wonder, too,' says she, with a shrug. 'Two people with two such tempers!'

'Has Tita a temper?' asks Marian indifferently.

Lady Rylton regards her curiously.

'Have you not found that out yet?' asks she.

'No,' coldly.

'It argues badly for you,' says her aunt, with a small, malicious smile. 'She has shown you none of it, then?'

'None,' distinctly.

'My dear Marian, I am afraid Maurice is proving false,' says Lady Rylton, leaning back in her chair, and giving way to soft, delicate mirth—the mirth that suits her Dresden china sort of beauty. 'Evidently our dear Tita is not *afraid* of you.'

'You take a wrong reading of it, perhaps,' says Mrs. Bethune, who is now, in spite of all her efforts to be emotionless, a little pale. 'She is simply so indifferent to Maurice, that she does not care whom he likes or dislikes—with whom he spends —or wastes his time. Or with whom he——'

'Flirts?' puts in Lady Rylton, lifting her brows; there is most insolent meaning in her tone.

For the first time Mrs. Bethune loses herself; she turns upon her aunt, her eyes flashing.

'Maurice does not flirt with me,' says she.

It seems horrible—*horrible*, that thought. Maurice—his love—it surely is hers! And to talk of it as a mere flirtation! Oh *no!* Her very soul seems to sink within her.

'My good child, who was speaking of you?' says Lady Rylton, with a burst of amusement. 'You should control yourself, my dear Marian. To give yourself away like that is to suffer defeat at any moment. One would think you were a girl in your first season, instead of being a mature married woman. Well, and if not with you, with whom does Maurice flirt?'

'With no one.' Marian has so far commanded herself as to be able now to speak collectedly. 'If you will keep to the word "flirtation," you must think of Tita, though perhaps "flirtation" is too mild a word to——'

'Tita!'

Tita's mother-in-law grows immediately interested.

'Yes, Tita. What 1 was going to say
when you interrupted me was, that she
refuses to take *me* into consideration—or
anyone else for the matter of that—
because——'

She stops — she feels choking ; she
honestly believes that Tita likes Tom
Hescott far more than she likes her
husband. But that the girl is guilty, even
in *thought* guilty, she does *not* believe ;
and now if she speaks—and to this woman
of all others—— And yet if she *does*
speak, ruin will probably come of it—to
Tita. She hesitates ; she is lost !

'Oh, go on !' says Lady Rylton, who
can be a little vulgar at times—where the
soul is coarse, the manner will be coarse
too.

'There is a cousin !' says Marian slowly.

'A cousin ? You grow interesting !'
says Lady Rylton. There is a silence for
a moment, and then : 'Do you mean to
tell me that this girl,' with a scornful
intonation, 'has a—— Really,' with a

shrug, 'considering her birth, one may be excused for calling it—a *follower* ?'

' Yes.'

' And so *l'ingénue* has awakened at last !'

' If you mean Tita,' icily, ' I think she is in love with her cousin ; and, beyond all doubt, her cousin is in love with her.'

' Birds of a feather !' says Lady Rylton. It has been plain to Marian for the past five minutes that her aunt has been keeping back her temper with some difficulty. Now it flames forth. ' The *insolence !*' cries she, between her teeth. ' That little half-bred creature ! Fancy—just *fancy*— her daring to be unfaithful to *my* son ! To marry a Rylton, and then bring a low intrigue into his family !' She turns furiously on Marian. ' Where is she ?'

' Tita ?'

' Yes. I must see her this moment— this *moment;* do you hear ?' The tyrannical nature of her breaks out now in a furious outburst. She would have liked to get

Tita in her grasp and crush her. She
rises. ' I wish to speak to her.'

' I should advise you to do no such
foolish thing,' says Mrs. Bethune, rising
too.

' *You* advise !—you ! Who are you ?'
says Lady Rylton insolently. ' When did
I ever ask for your advice, or take it ?
Send that girl here—directly.'

' Surely you forget that " that girl " is at
this moment your hostess !' says Marian
Bethune, who has some sense of decency
left. ' This is her house ; I could not
deliver such a message to her.'

' Then take another ! Say——'

' Nor any other. She dislikes me, as I
dislike her. If you wish to see her, send
a message through her maid, or,' a happy
thought coming to her, ' through Margaret ;
she cares for Tita as a cat might care for
her kitten !'

' Poor Margaret,' says Lady Rylton,
with a sneer. ' I fear she will always have
to care for other cats' kittens !'

'Do you? I don't,' says Marian, who'
though she detests most people, has always
a strange tenderness for Margaret.

'What do you mean?' asks Lady Rylton
sharply.

'I think she will marry Colonel Neilson.'

'Don't make yourself more absurd than
you need be!' says her aunt contemptuously. 'An old maid like that! What
could Colonel Neilson see in her? I
don't believe a word of that ridiculous
story. Why, she is nearly as bad—*worse*,
indeed,' with a short laugh, 'than a widow
—like you!'

'I think she will marry him, for all that,'
says Mrs. Bethune calmly, with supreme
self-control. She takes no notice of her
insult.

'You can think as you like,' says her
aunt. 'There, go away; I must arrange
about seeing that girl.'

END OF VOL. II.

BILLING AND SONS, PRINTERS, GUILDFORD.